Cleanup on Aisle Geek

Sarah Blynne

For Paul and Amanda, my favorite geeks.

Hide Away – Daya
Girls Just Want to Have Fun – Cyndi Lauper
Hang On Sloopy – The McCoys
Cut to the Feeling – Carly Rae Jepsen
Not a Bad Thing – Justin Timberlake
willow. – Taylor Swift
Fantasy – Mariah Carey
Wild Thing – The Troggs
Candy – Mandy Moore
I Gotta Feeling – Black Eyed Peas
Would I Lie to You? – Eurythmics
Gimme Gimme Gimme – ABBA
Something Just Like This – Coldplay and The Chainsmokers
Beautiful Things - Benson Boone
Stay – Rihanna feat. Mikky Ekko
The Chain – Fleetwood Mac
You're No Good – Linda Ronstadt
Wait For You – Elliott Yamin
Is It Any Wonder? – Keane
. . .Baby One More Time – Britney Spears
Thank God – Kane Brown
Time of My Life – Bill Medley and Jennifer Warnes

Chapter 1

Nichole

It's a sad day when you have to consume a large amount of alcohol to get through a date.

Today is one of them. I'm halfway into a bottle of wine, and this date still sucks.

I thought I won the lottery when I met Trevor at a 5K in Seattle. I mean, I was wearing a Wonder Woman outfit with a pink tutu, for goodness' sake. He asked me out when we finished the run in twenty minutes, never batting an eye at the costume. He had a gleaming-white smile that reached his ocean-blue eyes that I found endearing, and a mop of blond hair that complemented them both.

Yeah, no. I lost the lottery on this one.

Allow me to catch you up on how this has gone.

He suggested a top-notch steak house in the city, and walked in wearing casual shorts and a sweatshirt. He hasn't once used basic manners with the waitstaff, has spent most of the evening talking about how he grew up in wealth without asking me a single question about myself, and I swear I just saw him gawking at a waitress's bubble butt. The ultimate blow came when I asked him what he was into, and I said I was a die-hard *Star Wars* fan. He brushed off the comment and called the franchise "overpaid and overrated." I've never wanted to punch someone more.

Whoever I met at that 5K is not the same guy sitting in front of me swirling a glass of whiskey and giving me a smolder like he's Fabio's twin.

"So," he says in what's intended to be a sexy voice paired with the look, though epically failing with both, "you're a house cleaner?"

"Yes." It isn't a funny question or answer, but the nervous, throaty giggles I've had the entire evening that make me sound like Santa Claus and the Joker appears again.

"That has to be hard. I can't imagine it pays very well." He takes a sip from his whiskey. "Didn't you say you have a child?"

I feel like he just slapped me five times in a row, but I paste on the Santa Claus giggle and carry on. "Yes?"

"Single mothers are always looking for someone to take care of them." Trevor wiggles a thoughtful finger at me. "They seek someone that can bring them financial security." He winks. "I could be that security for you and your son. You'd be one happy woman."

All I manage to do is nod and force myself to laugh to the point where it gives me a headache, and I'm shocked he hasn't noticed. I'm an embarrassment to society right now.

I down the rest of the glass of wine, praying to sweet baby Jesus that the buzz kicks in soon. I can't wait to tell my best friends about this doozy of a date when I get home.

"You've had quite a bit of wine tonight," Trevor remarks. "Maybe you should cut back."

Great, now he thinks I'm a raging alcoholic, and he has no clue that he's the source of my drinking urges. Maybe I should consider alcoholism as a way out of crappy dates. Or as a career choice.

Note to self: When I start thinking about drinking more, it's time to leave.

I feign a yawn. "I'm really tired. I think I need to head home."

"Oh." He has the nerve to look shocked. "Okay. Let me walk you to your car."

"You don't have to—"

"No trouble." He tosses a few bills on the table and escorts me out.

Trevor had told me he was taking me to a fancy French restaurant in Seattle, and that I should dress my best. I spent way too much time doing my makeup and hair. Becca and Taryn have been my best friends for so long that they knew I needed help the moment they stepped into my apartment. I really would've had more fun staying home with my son and watching him play *Fortnite*.

I feel like an idiot for spending so much time fretting over this date, only to find it to be a bust. Like all my dates this past year.

Which, to be honest, have all been worse than this one.

Allow me to relay some examples.

1. One guy I met on a dating app took me snowboarding and kept making weird eye contact with me while sensually massaging his board.

2. I met another guy who lived across the street from a client's house. On our date, he asked me what a

woman of color was. I'm *Black*.

3. I went on a bowling date with a guy who kept calling me by his ex's name, and my name was on the freaking screen.

4. Oh, and this one's the kicker. One man I met at Creekside's coffee shop, Caffeinated Vino, brought me to a romantic restaurant that he said was his favorite. A woman burst in and said she's his wife. I had zero clue that he was married.

So, yeah, I've had some terrible luck in the dating world. Tonight is further proof of that.

Trevor walks me to my car, his last shot at being a gentleman. I fish for my keys in my Grogu purse, relieved that I get to spend the rest of my night in peace.

"All right, thank—"

I don't get to finish, because Trevor is sticking his tongue down my throat.

Ew. Ew. EW. WHAT IS HAPPENING?!

I push him away, but he keeps an arm locked around my waist as he continues to assault my mouth. All my time spent in Pilates and running marathons pays off when I shove him so hard he stumbles. Then add a good slap to that stupidly smooth and luminous face of his.

"What are you doing?" I can't even push out my Santa-Joker laugh. I'm just downright shocked.

He shrugs nonchalantly like we're just talking about the steak we ate at the restaurant. "What? I was giving you a good night kiss!"

"No! No." I wiggle a warning finger at him. "No good night kisses. No tonguing, licking, kissing, anything with the mouth! Not today, Satan!" My heels clack on the pavement as I round to my car. "Thank God I drove myself!"

"I thought women liked it when the *man* made the first move!" he shouts, as if he deserves the title.

"I'll be making the first move when I block you, you pervert!" I yank open my car door. "Have a nice night!"

I double-check that my doors are locked, and immediately go to block Trevor in everything imaginable: dating apps, social media, all the things. Unfortunately, it's not the first time I've had to do this.

I stare blankly at the Grogu air freshener hanging from my rearview mirror. I've been divorced for eight years, and just within the last year, I finally felt ready to move on. I didn't think I could trust anyone ever again. However, I didn't think dating at thirty-three would be so hard. I have a strong hope that the next person I meet will be different than my cheating ex-husband. I have faith that that person will be wonderful, romantic, sweet, caring, and of course, sexy as all get-out. Something's changed in the dating world, and I can't put a finger on it.

Oh, I know what it is. It *sucks*.

After what feels like an hour, I lift up my head to text Becca and Taryn.

Me: Why do men suck?

I play Kane Brown in the background in my car that lived with the dinosaurs as I drive home, taking in the scenery of the small town at night. Fall has arrived and it's getting colder, which means darkness early in the afternoon, and darkness through the morning. But it also makes for pretty scenery.

All the streetlamps and trees gradually shifting to fall colors give the pathways between businesses their own cheer. A movie theater, a froyo place, the only coffee shop in a five-mile radius, a clothing store for rich people, a phở restaurant, a Target, and a hardware store all make up the clock-formed shopping area of Landing Plaza. Appropriately named due to Boeing Field being right across the street.

I pull into the parking spot in front of my fourplex up the hill from Landing Plaza. I stare blankly at the view of Creekside, a flat field of city lights, three small neighborhoods (one of which is basically all apartments), and a light mist from the rain. You'd think I've been able to muster up courage to answer the "how did the date go?" conversation that people always ask, but the pitiful looks I get are sadder than my whole life.

My phone pings multiple times.

Becca: Women have been asking that question for decades.
Taryn: Oh crap, what happened?
Becca: Yes, that too. What happened?

What happened indeed.

Me: I'll tell you later. I need to go to bed and sleep for a million hours.

My phone is blowing up by the time I turn my car off.

Becca: A million hours sounds excellent, Felicia.

Taryn: I vote we do shots. Felicia Becca, you can hook us up with free alcohol.

You're probably wondering what this "Felicia" nonsense is. You see, "bye Felicia" was a common funny phrase that made a comeback years ago. Every time Becca, Taryn, and I made a retort or comment, we would end it with "Becky" or "Susan" or "Carol," and yes, "Felicia," just because it always made our comment sound funnier. Eventually, we only called each other "Felicia," and it stuck ever since. Does it make sense? Absolutely not. But there's no dialing down the crazy.

Becca: We'll see. I may have used up my allotted free drinks this week.

Taryn: We got an alcoholic up in here!

Becca: Hey, it's been a rough week. Customers are dumb and I'm still single.

I snort at the text exchange that has gone completely off topic. I can always rely on them to make me laugh and reassure me that I'm crazy, but only in the best way.

Me: We can be alcoholics together. Good night, my Felicias.

I trudge to my fourplex and knock slowly on my neighbor's door. God, even my knocks sound out my despair.

Camilla opens the door and I smell Mexican food immediately. "Oh hi, Nichole!" She always pronounces my name *nee-cole* due to her accent. "The boys are playing video games in Oscar's bedroom." She eyes me up and down, and sees my pathetically downcast face. "Oh no, did your date not go well?"

Oh boy. I didn't even have to say anything and she's noticed something is wrong.

I shake my head. "I had a lot more fun when I got in a car accident with my ex-husband ten years ago."

"Oh, lo siento, chica." She opens the door wider to let me into her apartment, and I can hear the boys shouting toward the back. "What happened?"

"Let's just say he's a rich pervert who thinks money is everything and simply being a man means he's allowed to stick his tongue down my throat." I shiver at the memory that just occurred minutes ago. "Unfortunately, that's not the worst date I've had."

Camilla gasps. "This is why I gave up on dating a long time ago. *¿Por qué los hombres son tan idiotas?*"

"I have no idea what you said, but I like how it ended."

Camilla and I have been friends for years, and I still don't know Spanish. Maybe I should pay attention in case there're some insults I can use.

She pats my arm. "I'll go get Kaden for you. It'll get better, mija, I promise. You're a beautiful, kind, amazing woman. You'll snatch someone soon. I may have given up on dating, but I believe there's more hope for you."

Whoever I end up with better not make fun of my Star Wars *fandom*, I think.

All I can hope is that she's right. Camilla has literally been the best neighbor I could've ever asked for. Any time I have to work late or have a date, or I can't take Kaden to school, she's been willing to help. Kaden and Oscar have become best friends because of that.

I don't know if that's sweet or sad.

As a fellow house cleaner, I have someone to take on clients I can't get to, or vice versa. And, because she grew up in Mexico in a large family, she always manages to make so much food that she gives the rest to me. Most of the time, I end up eating it since Kaden doesn't have a sophisticated palate yet.

Once I settle in bed, I keep replaying the events of the failed date. Then I look back on when we met, and why I didn't see the warning signs from the beginning. I thought I was more careful about looking out for red flags. I must have missed something.

The problem is there has to be a measure of trust somewhere. That trust is built and established whenever I'm texting or talking on the phone with the person. As time goes on, they always seem a legit person. A *real* person. Then, on the date, a Jekyll and Hyde switch flips, and they obliterate that trust in seconds. All it takes is them asking me an insulting question or forcing themselves on me.

That was Trevor. He shielded his true self so I wouldn't see who he really was.

Idiota.

Lunch. Check.

Backpack. Check.

Homework. Che—

Shoot, it's on the kitchen table.

I dig around the plethora of papers and art on the table for Kaden's homework that's due today. Man, this table is so dirty. There're marker and crayon marks all over the wood, and I'm pretty sure my carpet underneath has turned into a new color from all the paint Kaden has dropped over the years. I haven't bothered to clean it yet. Let's be honest, my son is ten years old. He's going to get it dirty again anyway.

Aha! There's his assignment.

Now in backpack. Check.

Ugh. I want to sleep. My crappy dating choices kept me awake for way too long last night. The fact that it's seven in the morning doesn't help at all. This warm cup of Joe usually does the trick, but I'll need more to get through today.

"Mom!" Kaden shouts down the hallway. He's digging through his lunch box. "You didn't pack my treat for the day!"

I grunt and riffle through my purse for something quick. I normally give him a little something sweet so he can enjoy his lunch more, but it slipped my mind. I love that kid to death, but I don't really care about the treat right now. He can sneak it out of someone else's lunch for all I care.

Lack of sleep on a single mom is not a good look.

I find a stick of gum and toss it in his open video-game themed lunch box. "There."

"That's not a treat!"

"It is when you don't feel like brushing your teeth."

"Does that mean I don't have to brush my teeth if I just chew gum?" he asks excitedly.

I chuckle and pat his cheek. Oh, how I love destroying his hopes of avoiding responsibility and basic hygiene. "No." I kiss him on the cheek and turn him around by the shoulders. I lightly push him in the direction of the hallway littered with clothes and toys. "Now hurry up, we're late."

By the time he finishes brushing his teeth, I book it to Creekside Elementary five minutes away, drop him off, and head to my first client of the day.

Chapter 2

Nichole

"I'm so sorry, Nichole, but is there any way you can work faster?" my client, Linda, asks as soon as I finish vacuuming her guest room.

I give her a tight-lipped smile and clasp my hands in front of me. She has a two-story house and wants me to work faster. Good luck with that, lady.

"Is there a problem?" I ask in my ultra-fake kind voice that I've learned to master with this job.

"I have guests coming in an hour, and I just wanted everything to be done by then." She whips her head around in a panic, her brunette Karen-haircut swishing around her. She scans the room to see if I made it as perfect as she requested—a request she made without even greeting me when I walked in. It was bad enough that I was running late this morning, and then she put me in an unrealistic time crunch.

Linda, unfortunately for her, is one of my least favorite clients. She comments on how I do my job (even though her house is already pretty clean), and finds my clothes "interesting" as I wear an old Grogu T-shirt and Grogu studded earrings. Yes. I know I'm a little obsessed. Whatever.

Linda points to the bed. "Have you washed the sheets yet?"

"No, I was just about to actually."

"We don't have time," she barks. "It's okay." She wiggles her hand at the bed. "You can just put clean sheets over those ones."

It legit takes every bit of my self-control to not ask her if she's lost her mind. "You want me to put clean sheets . . . over the unwashed ones?"

"Yeah. They won't know the difference."

I quirk an eyebrow. Apparently, playing host makes her lose a marble or five. "Why don't I just change the sheets and throw them in the washer?" I ask with as level a tone as possible.

"No, I don't want to have to do laundry when they're here. And I don't want any laundry left in the washer or dryer."

This woman is going to be the death of me. This goes against any and all cleaning standards I have. I have no cheat codes when it comes to cleaning. Good thing I'm a mother, because I can avert a crisis like nothing ever happened.

I lift my hand to bargain with her. "Tell you what. I'll take the sheets to my house and wash them. Your guests won't see any laundry that needs to be done, it takes the pressure off you, and you'll get clean sheets on the bed."

Linda seems pleased with this offer, even though it involves more work for me. "Are you sure?"

I paste on a fake, bright smile to hide my annoyance. No, I'm really not sure, but I just want her to shut up. "Positive."

She sighs in relief. "Thank you. *Thank you.* You'd be helping me a *ton!*" She holds up a finger. "Let me give you some cash. It's the least I can do for the extra help."

When she turns and heads down the hallway, I smile for real and chuck my fist in the air.

I have sixteen clients overall. I clean between two and four houses per day.

I'm kept plenty busy. By some miracle, I manage to pay our bills for our small two-bedroom apartment and for anything Kaden needs. For the most part, I get home around early evening, when Kaden and Oscar are usually skateboarding outside. Becca said she would be home before me and Camilla, so she promised to keep an eye out and make sure they don't kill themselves. Her words, not mine.

Kaden and Oscar move on to playing in Kaden's room when I get home, because they know I'm prepping a fancy, homemade box of mac and cheese for dinner: A single mom's dream come true.

I mean, ahem . . . a *little boy*'s dream come true.

As I wait for the water to boil, I decide to get my Grogu headphones and watch *The Mandalorian* while I cook. I usually leave them on an end table in the living room so I can grab them quickly.

Yet, I can't find them.

I search the other table next to the couch. Not there.

Not on the kitchen counters.

Not on the dining room table.

Not in my purse.

Then I go to my bedroom, because I don't usually put them anywhere else. I have a nightstand on each side of my queen bed, and they're not there either.

I even dig through my Grogu collection in the corner of my room. I'm in love with all the stuffed Grogus of all shapes and sizes, and they take up nearly half my bedroom. Becca and Taryn think I need an intervention with all the Grogu things I have. I have *a lot*.

Crap! They're not there either.

I groan in frustration and tilt my head back. Then I see them.

Taped to my freaking ceiling.

"Are you kidding me?!" I shout. When I hear the silly giggles of little boys in Kaden's room, I immediately know who the culprits are. "I can't reach that high!"

"Use the Force!" Kaden shouts, and Oscar is practically dying laughing. How dare he use *Star Wars* against me.

"*You* use the Force, *child*!" I shout back, and take a picture to send to my friends. "Get them down, please!"

My phone pings when I get back to the kitchen.

Taryn: This is why you shouldn't have had a boy.

Becca: Because she had so much control over that, Felicia.

Taryn: Sure she did. She could've just told the fetus she wanted it to be a girl.

Me: You guys are ridiculous.

"Here, Mom," Kaden says a few minutes later with my headphones in his palm. I snatch them from his grip with a grumble, and he just laughs. Stinking kid.

Becca: What's for dinner?
Me: Mac and cheese.
Taryn: homemade or from a box?
Me: what do you think?
Becca: save some for me k thanksssssss.
Taryn: Me too. I don't feel like cooking.

Not only am I lucky to have Camilla as my neighbor, but Becca and Taryn also happen to live in the same fourplex. All three of us wanted the apartment I live in now, but once they heard my pity story about being a newly divorced single mom, they withdrew their applications and let me have it. We ended up sitting in the middle of the empty living room of the apartment and talked for hours. Taryn was the quiet one at first. Subdued. She watched Becca and me hit it off immediately, since we're both so quirky and love to love. Taryn eventually relaxed and started talking, even making dirty jokes. We've been best friends ever since. Once two more apartments opened up, Becca and her brother Parker moved in above me to the right, and Taryn took the unit just above me, just so we could all be together. It's been a blessing.

Me: I'm feeding two boys! I may not have any left!
Taryn: I'll search your freezer then.

While the pasta boils, I move to the sink to do the dishes. I have no dishwasher, so all dishes have to be hand-washed. It's Kaden's least favorite chore. Why I didn't have him do this is beyond me.

Well, the moment I turn the faucet on, I get the feeling it's his retaliation to dish duty. Water from the attached hose sprays directly at my face and drenches my chest. I shriek and sputter and shake my head everywhere until I have enough sense to turn off the faucet. I'm gasping from the shock as I inspect the assault hose.

Only to find a rubber band tied around the sprayer.

"Boys!" I scream.

All I hear is the laughter of two boys who successfully pranked me. Again.

I tread down the hall a couple steps, chuckling humorlessly. "You're really testing my patience, children!" I shout at Kaden's closed door. Needless to say, this is the gist of how my nights go.

When I finish the mac and cheese, I yell that dinner is ready. The boys barrel down the hallway and footsteps pound all over the kitchen. Oddly, Oscar is holding a pack of Oreos in his hands. A pack that I bought yesterday and couldn't find today.

"Hold on!" I hold up my hand to stop them and motion to the cookies. "Did you eat those?"

The boys shake their heads. I snatch the package and see that they've been opened, but the cookies are all there, and they look fine. They're trying so hard not to smile. There's another prank at play, yet I'm too tired to figure out what it is.

"Put them on the counter, and don't touch them till after dinner."

The kids help themselves to my "homemade" dinner, and we eat together like a very odd, mixed family.

The boys finish eating and retrieve the pack of Oreos. Kaden hands me two of them. "Here."

I'm super suspicious of him, but I take them anyway. Because I always doubt my gut instinct. Which might be why I'm still single.

Anyway.

I like a little something sweet to eat after dinner. They race to Kaden's room with their laughter echoing in the hallway.

One bite, and I've fallen victim to another prank.

The Oreos have toothpaste in them.

I dart to the kitchen and spit out the cookie in the sink. "Are you kidding me right now?"

Once I've rinsed out my mouth thoroughly, I stomp down the hallway. Unfortunately, this doesn't count as brushing my teeth.

I burst through the door and Oscar screams like a little girl.

"Get the Husk Monster!" Kaden shouts as he throws a pillow at me.

"We're innocent!" Oscar yells and climbs onto the bed with Kaden.

I lean against the doorway and decide to make this interesting. "If you do the dishes, Husk Monster will do nothing." I wink at them. The ultimate payback.

Oscar leans back to whisper to Kaden, "Is she serious?"

"Yes." I toss the pillow back onto the bed. "I made dinner. You do dishes." I clap twice. "Come on. Husk Monster waits for no one."

Five days after the pompous *Star Wars*-hater debacle, I started to think there was some hope when a thirty-year-old named Nick messaged me through Beeline, a popular dating app. I decided to give it a try, considering that apparently men at 5K runs cannot be trusted. I told him after messaging back and forth for hours that we should meet up for a drink. To my surprise, he agreed.

So here I am at a famous brewery in Seattle by the baseball stadium, looking at the front doors every ten seconds to see if he's come in. From the photo in his dating profile, Nick had thick-framed glasses with blond hair longer on one side that was combed back. A total '90s look, but still so sexy. He's also an uncle to three nieces that he loves to death—an ultimate plus.

Finally, after the five hundredth time of peeking at the doors, a man that looks relatively similar to his dating photo comes in, searching the bustling place for someone that I'm hoping is me. I get his attention when I wave at him. Once he sees me, the sparkle in his eyes fades and his shoulders drop. He doesn't seem thrilled. At all. If anything, he now looks appalled.

"Uh . . ." His mouth hangs open as he approaches the table I saved for us. "I'm sorry. I can't do this."

He must be married and just came to his senses. That would be just my luck. "What—"

"I thought you were a lot prettier." He shakes his head as I take my turn dropping my jaw. "I don't want to waste your time." He turns and walks back to the door, and I'm stunned beyond belief. Which flips to rage in seconds.

"Well aren't *you* generous?!" I yell after him as he exits. Talk about a punch to the gut.

The next day after that raging insult, I got a message through Beeline from someone else. Keith, from Bothell, twenty-nine, dark hair and dark stubble, and a smolder that could melt Superman's costume. I've been sitting on the couch messaging him for the last fifteen minutes, and it hasn't gone to hell just yet. I like to be optimistic.

Me: If you claim to be a Star Wars lover, what's your most prized possession?

Keith: Oh I'll show you a prized possession.

I wait a few moments and expect him to show me a real lightsaber signed by Mark Hamill or a LEGO Grogu. Not going to lie, something signed by Mark Hamill would be impressive.

I get a message, and it's not at all what I expected. Keith had the nerve to send me a photo of . . . something very much not related to *Star Wars*.

Something located south of the face, and unsolicited, if you get my drift.

I shriek and throw my phone across the room, crashing it into a DVD bookshelf. Whelp, that derailed faster than Thomas the Train on a bad day.

A week after the not-*Star-Wars*-related photo fiasco, I went to a Starbucks on the way to a client in Kirkland where a handsome young store manager named Landon wrote his phone number on the cup. I thought it was charming, so of course I hit him up. Before I knew it, we arranged to have brunch before I went to the same client's house the following week.

As usual, I get there early, so I pass the time by ordering coffee and toast. Probably not the best combination, but better than nothing while I scroll through my phone.

"Are you Nichole Tyler?"

A manly voice almost has me nearly jumping out of my seat and splattering coffee on the table. I hope this isn't my date, because that was *not* graceful.

This overweight, bearded man who reeks of pot and dressed in ratty sweats is definitely not my date.

"Yes?"

The man, eyes half-lidded and dazed, hands me a folded piece of paper. "Landon wanted me to give you this," he says in a lazy voice. "Have a nice day." He turns and leaves before I can ask any questions.

What the crap is happening?

I open the note.

Sorry, I'm not gonna make it. My wife says you're not our type. —Landon

His *wife*? Did she stalk me on social media for photos?

I just can't even.

Once again, men never seem to fail to leave me completely stunned. Not once did I get the vibe that I might be talking to a swinger.

I crumple the note, throw it on the floor, and finish my coffee in silence.

Three drinks in at The Cheesecake Factory, south of Creekside, and Aaron still hasn't shown up. It's been forty-five minutes, and I've been drinking by myself at the bar. Just when I didn't think my dating life could resemble a train wreck even more . . .

"Your date still hasn't shown up?" the bartender asks. His name tag says Blake. Or Baker. Or Blaze. My vision isn't all there.

"Nope," I mumble with my cheek resting on my palm. "Men suck. I suck."

"I'm sure that's not true," he consoles me. "I mean, men suck, but I doubt you do."

I chuckle. "You're sweet." My unfocused eyes rake him from head to waist, the bar blocking the bottom half of his body. "And cute. I think?" I shake my head. "The last three weeks have been one dating disaster after another. I think that earns me a night of drinking."

"I would agree if you weren't about to fall asleep on the bar."

He's right. I should stop drinking. But my self-esteem and confidence have taken a nosedive to the bottom of a rocky mountain and it's going to burst into flames if I go on another date soon.

Nope. I'm going to drink.

"Fill 'er up, Baker," I say when I knock the shot glass against the counter.

"It's Blake, actually."

I pound my fist on the counter and point at him. "Ha! I knew it!"

My head aches so much it feels like it's inflating. It might explode at any moment.

Good thing I didn't wake up on someone's porch or on the floor. I don't remember a single thing after finding out Blake's name. It's literally a miracle I even managed to get up for work.

I can't wait to come home and throw up again.

A text from Becca is a shameful summary.

Becca: Because you asked me in your drunken state to remind you of what happened last night, the bartender called me to pick you up. Apparently, he became your drinking buddy. You were laughing at nothing, sort of like a psychopath. Then I had to pull over so you could throw up. Then you passed out.

Okay, I don't remember any of that. I don't even recall asking her to remind me what happened. I'm kind of regretting that now.

Man, I'm a nightmare when I'm drunk.

Me: I'm so, so sorry.

Becca: Oh well. I'm just glad you didn't drive. It makes for a funny story when you're not feeling like death.

Me: If it was anyone else, I'd wanna crawl in a corner and die.

Becca: Well you can do that later. I'll bring you coffee in a bit.

Me: I love you so much.

Becca: Another thing you said repeatedly last night.

I put my phone in the cupholder and groan. I should've just taken a sick day. I'm in a constant state of nauseousness and my head is an incessant hammer behind my eyes.

A fast-food sign pops up at a freeway exit, and I swear it's a sign from God. I take the exit and race to the drive-thru like my life depends on it. Right now, it feels like it. I feel just a smidge better that I may find relief until a text from an unwanted nemesis pops up on my phone.

Jared: Hey babe, call me when you get a chance.

I have to hold back vomit just reading my ex-husband's text. He calls me "babe" like some chick magnet. And for some reason, I had a child with him.

I might as well bite the bullet. I'm already dying anyway.

"Hey, babe." His flirtatious, deep voice is making me more nauseous. It's a wonder how I at one point fell in love with that sound.

"First off, don't call me babe," I say softly so nothing will rise to my throat. "What do you need? I'm on my way to a client's house and I feel like death on a stick, so make it snappy."

He huffs. "So, here's the thing. I would love to see Kaden this summer as usual, and I know I'm supposed to buy his plane tickets. But I got myself into some debt that I really need to pay off, otherwise I'm not going to be able to afford my rent and I'll have to move."

Crap. I don't like where this is going.

"I need you to get his ticket this time."

I drop my jaw. Our lawyers did not make that arrangement in our divorce. I kept Kaden for the school year, Jared always got him for the summer. "Are you freaking kidding me, Jared? A ticket to Wichita is at least five hundred dollars! I don't have that kind of money!"

"I know, I know, but I want to be able to have a home for Kaden to come to. It'll just be a while before I get this paid off and I know I can't get his ticket right now."

Another reminder of why I'm glad we got divorced: He was horrible with money. He was always seeking a thrill, only to bring us into debt. Before Kaden was in the picture, we moved into his parents' house. That was a nightmare. The months I spent watching his dad scratch his butt with a spatula and his mom criticizing my cooking were months I wish never happened.

I also wish the affair he had with his assistant eight years ago never happened either. Otherwise, I wouldn't have needed to feel ready to date again.

"Please, Nicnic," he begs.

He used to call me that when we were married. Now it's nails on a chalkboard. "That's not allowed either."

"Well, I don't know what else to do!"

"Well what did you do to get yourself into so much debt that you can't set aside a few bucks every month?"

Jared sighs. "I had mold issues in my bathroom that led to water leaks showing up on my ceiling, so I had to have the bathroom gutted and the ceiling repaired. Then the transmission on my car went kaput. On top of that, I had to get my roof repaired. It's . . . been a lot."

Despite the past with him being a man whore, Jared's been a good dad to Kaden. He always finds a way to spend time with him. He's not trying to avoid seeing his son; he just can't afford it this time. Shockingly, his reasons are valid.

"You do realize this means I have to work *more*?" I ask sharply.

"Well, you'll make extra money to put into your savings." I can *hear* the nonchalant shrug in his voice.

"Are *you* seriously giving me financial advice?"

"No, no. Just trying to help you see the positive side."

The nerve of this man. "*Positive*? Bruh, you be smokin' something strong if you think there's a positive side here."

"Look, either you buy his ticket, or you don't have a free summer. That's what it's come down to."

Free summer. He's right. I love Kaden with all my heart, pranks and all. I'd be lying if I said I don't love having the apartment to myself for two and a half months. It's the equivalent to getting a massage from angels. When he comes back, I feel refreshed and ready to take on another year with just the two of us.

I sigh long and deep. "Okay, Jared. I'll pay for it. But I'm not doing it for you."

His sigh of relief is audible. "Thank you. Thank you, babe. You're the best."

I hang up on him. Despite not being married to that pasty White boy for a long time, he still gets on my nerves.

I park my ancient car in my client's driveway and stare blankly at the house. It's a quaint one-story with a gorgeous front yard and a super cute porch with a couple rocking chairs. It's a simple, small home, yet they pay me well, and even tip me. From the sounds of it, I'll need to find ways to get my clients to pay me more. Maybe do stuff that they don't need done "just because."

Can't believe this is what my life has become.
Jesus, take the whole car.

Chapter 3

Nichole

Taryn: Mama needs a drink.

Me: Funny you say that while I'm scrubbing a toilet.

Becca: I just gagged a little, thank you.

Taryn: I just got done conducting the worst interview I've ever had with the stupidest person on the planet that someone referred to me for some reason! Not to mention I'm swamped with other work and my boss is still a moron.

Becca: and I've been dealing with having to repeatedly remake orders 'cause a barista isn't putting in the orders right. I could use some booze. Let's get crunk.

Becca: I mean, not totally crunk 'cause, you know, we have to adult.

I flush the toilet I just cleaned, and I watch the water twirl and drown, just like my love life. I haven't tried dating for a week. My sorrow drinking with the bartender was the last attempt. My shame hasn't worn off yet.

Me: count me in. I haven't told you guys all the details of my crappier than crap dates the last couple weeks, and my ex-husband called and I want to throttle him.

Becca: more reasons to drink.

Caffeinated Vino is my favorite and most convenient coffee shop in town, and also where Becca works as a barista. A coffee bar on one side opens early in the morning, then the cocktail bar on the other side opens around dinnertime. By then, both bars are available to everyone for coffee or drinks till late in the evening. Mood lighting leaves bright specks in the ceiling, giving the place a dim and romantic feel. Fairy lights border all the windows and fake leaves stick to the glass to complete the fall atmosphere. Perfect for after-work cocktails that your best friend can get you for a hefty discount.

When we Felicias meet here once a week for drinks, we have a specific booth where we always sit, right in the middle of the cafe next to a laser-cut wall panel that separates the coffee bar from the cocktail bar. Sitting in the middle gives us access to both bars when either one is open. In this small town, everyone in Creekside knows that the Felicias sit here.

"So this person was referred to me," Taryn begins her story, leaning close so we can all hear, her wavy, mahogany hair nearly falling into her whiskey sour as she takes a sip, then waves down a waiter. "Can y'all get me a refill? Thank you so much." He nods and walks away, then she leans in to continue her story. "She wore slippers and sweatpants to the interview, then proceeded to say she insists on being comfortable at work. Then, she says she refuses to work at a place that doesn't have a coffee machine. I told her we have a Keurig." Taryn slaps the table, the rings on all her fingers doubling the noise. "She had the audacity to get up and walk out!"

Becca's jaw drops. "In the middle of the interview?"

"Yup!" She sighs. "Whatever. It's the way my life goes. Something always goes wrong."

My Santa-Joker laugh comes out, but not because it's funny. It's just that stupid. A lot of inconveniences happen to Taryn, but instead of laughing it off, she pities herself. She's not all wrong in feeling that way, though. I just wish good things would happen for her for once.

"People like that make me want to drink more," Becca comments. "We have a customer that's basically a mocha Nazi."

I nod. "Oh yeah, isn't it Russel? The guy with the Russian accent and huge, scraggly beard?"

"Yeah. He returned his mocha *three times.*" Becca practically snarls as she shakes her head. "I would've just drank all of them if he hadn't sipped from each cup. Or if they didn't all have dairy."

"Dairy is delicious," Taryn says. "So worth it."

"Dairy milk is gross. Cheese is another story." Becca peers over my shoulder toward the entrance. "Felicia Taryn, I think your boy toy is here," she says with a lilt.

Taryn smacks Becca on the arm when I turn around and see her other best friend, Knox Bentley, walk in. We constantly joke with Taryn that they're going to get married someday. She flat-out insists they're just super close friends since they met at Taryn's last job. Someone who is a close friend doesn't always quit their job and decide to work as a waiter just to live closer to their best girl friend.

Can you see why neither Becca nor I believe her?

I'm not going to lie, Knox is hot. Like, drop-dead hot. He's the epitome of sharpness in his navy-blue suit and gray tie. His bronze complexion matches Taryn's, with a light beard and tattoos along his neck and chest, his hair is a tightly coiled chestnut bush, and his dimples make all the women swoon. Except Taryn, apparently. She's usually the third wheel on dates with his girlfriend, Katie, an obnoxious, high-maintenance *Barbie* blonde. That's the only shadow of proof we have that they're simply just best friends.

Knox approaches our table and Taryn gets up from the booth. "Hey, ladies. I don't wanna interrupt, it'll just be a second." He looks at her. "I'm offering a free hug in place of your crappy day."

"Aw, you're the best," Taryn squeals and hugs him. Becca and I give each other the side-eye. The way he sways her body back and forth, holding her longer than a usual friendly hug, he's definitely not just a friend. Neither one of them will admit it, though.

"Thank you," Taryn mumbles into his shoulder before letting him go. "You have a date with Katie?"

"Yeah, I'm on my way to pick her up. Just wanted to stop by on the way, make sure you're okay."

I glance at Becca again, who's giving me a dubious look. To which I nod.

My heart falls. Taryn would be one lucky woman if she ended up with Knox. He's hung out with us occasionally, and he's genuinely the kindest, most chill guy I've ever met. He and Taryn have a load of inside jokes that crack each other up, and he's always been there for her. He always seems to know when she needs support, even when she doesn't ask for it. She's someone who seems to need it a lot.

I want a guy like Knox.

"Have fun," he says to Taryn as he turns to leave. "Good to see you ladies."

Taryn sits back in the booth and I give her the stink eye. "Just admit you have a thing for him already."

She rolls her eyes. "I don't."

"Then he's definitely got a thing for you, 'cause he stopped by on the way to his date just to give you a *hug*," Becca points out. "You guys should talk about that."

She laughs bitterly. "That's never gonna happen 'cause there ain't nothing to talk about."

"Denial, denial, denial," Becca singsongs.

Something about the mystery of Taryn's and Knox's emotions for each other makes it so much sweeter and more romantic. *Great.* I'm depressed again.

"Oh yeah, you were gonna tell us about your date," Becca says, turning to me. "What happened?"

"*Dates*," I correct her.

"So my picking you up at The Cheesecake Factory incident wasn't the only one?" Becca asks as if this is news to her.

"Say what now?" Taryn pipes up.

"She was doing shots with the bartender and couldn't drive home." Becca laughs. "Our Felicia is a funny drunk."

"I got stood up. I had a right to get wasted."

"You should've called me!" Taryn exclaims. "I would've done some sympathy shots with you!"

"Wasn't that kind of night," Becca whispers loudly.

"Oh, you guys haven't heard the half of it." I down the rest of my lemon drop. "Before that, I was unknowingly being set up with swingers—"

Becca nearly spits out her drink.

"Before *that*, I was talking to someone on Beeline who sent me unsolicited photos of . . . things."

Both women groan.

"Before *that*, the guy walked in, said he thought I would be prettier, then walked out."

Taryn wears a hard scowl, but Becca's eyes are bulging out of her head. "Oh. My. God."

"On top of that, Jared called and said he needs me to pay for Kaden's plane ticket this summer. I need money."

"You need a *vacation*," Becca adds.

"You need a man," Taryn says.

Becca wags a finger. "Now that's what I need."

"Is Shawn still trying to talk to you?" I ask. Shawn is Becca's ex-boyfriend from her teen years that, for the last week, has been insistent on talking to her "just to catch up." She's been hesitant, to say the least. It took almost a year for her to recover from the breakup.

"Today, actually." She shrugs. "He's never been good with being single. Ever since we broke up, he's always been with *someone*. At least that's what it looks like when I look up his Facebook."

"You stalk your ex-boyfriend?" Taryn asks with surprise.

"Don't act like you've never done it before."

"I don't," Taryn corrects her. "I couldn't care less what my exes are doing. My single status is my business."

"Maybe that's what I need to do. Be single." I shake my head. "Screw it. I'm done with men."

Becca frowns. "No you're not."

"Yes, I am." I blow out a sigh. "I thought I was ready to trust men again. A *good* man. But, if the last few dates have been any indication, there's no such thing as a good man." I fight back tears. "It's like no one sees me as worthy of being dating material because I'm a single mom."

Becca shakes her head. "I don't think that's it at all."

I sniffle. "Sure feels like it."

"No. No crying while sober." Becca winks. "We drink, *then* we cry."

Becca leaves her seat and heads to the bar to order more drinks, tying her dark blonde hair back in a ponytail as she smiles at the bartender. I take a few deep breaths to regain my composure and wipe the tears from my eyes. This shouldn't be bothering me so much, but when men attack my appearance and self-worth, it's tough to ignore the way it bruises me inside.

"It's just been a hard year so far," Taryn reassures me. "People don't always find 'The One' that soon."

"A year of being on numerous dates and finding duds and perverts!" I groan in frustration. "I literally can't trust anyone anymore. I need to go back to the circle where I wasn't ready to trust anyone, focus on being Kaden's mom, and stop having any expectations of meeting someone good."

"The problem is you've been looking online," Taryn says while Becca returns with drinks. "That's where all the pedophiles live."

Becca points at Taryn. "What she said."

"Only two of those guys were online, Felicias! I met one at Starbucks and another from one of my clients. I did meet one guy at the 5K that I thought was a winner."

Becca's eyebrows shoot up. "The one where you wore that Wonder Woman costume? That outfit shows off the contours of your butt. Any man would be all over that!"

"It means I'm fun and I have a nice butt!" I say with a neck roll. "It just attracts the wrong guys."

"This will sound weird coming from me," Becca warns, "but you have to trust that the right man will see everything that there is to love about you. Especially your butt."

"Shake that thang," Taryn adds while sipping her drink and shimmying. Becca adds a "boom boom boom" and all of us are laughing.

Becca bringing up that I have to trust that the right man will come along . . . If I can't trust men, trusting fate seems equally risky. Relying on that to guide my life doesn't seem like a good option.

But, shoot, I don't have a choice.

Man, do I need coffee. And I need it yesterday.

I don't have a client till eleven, but I still have to get up and make sure my child is being obedient by getting dressed and ready. When I go to pack his lunch because I didn't feel like doing it the night before, I find that the only food I have has to be warmed up. Good Lord, I need to go grocery shopping.

I check the lunch menu to see if they'll serve anything he'll eat. Pizza with a side of veggies. Good enough.

Kaden comes down the hall. I stuff a few dollar bills in his pocket. "For lunch."

"Yay," he says sleepily. I know he likes school lunch food. Lord knows why. For all I know, it's full of plastic and recycled rabbits.

"Okay, you got everything." I throw a beanie on his head as the final touch. "I'll see ya later. Love you."

"Love you."

He goes next door to ride with Oscar, and I have about an hour and a half to spare. I'm going to spend it in my bed.

That ends up being a mistake, though, because I wake up later than I expected to. Waking up mid-nap is only going to make today that much more exhausting, especially with the gray clouds and rain we always see in fall.

Time for a visit to Caffeinated Vino. Becca understands my struggle; she gives me free coffee from her discount if I'm in distress. And makes it priority coffee.

I make it to there at 10:30. I have to be at my client's in half an hour. The lobby is bustling with customers. Some go around me as they leave, only with more people pouring in. See, that would be fine and dandy, except for the fact that there's *a line that reaches the door.*

I'm bouncing on my feet and wringing my hands as if that's going to help this extremely indecisive customer ahead of me make up their freaking mind. I've seen her here before; she has a list of customizations for every. Single. Drink.

One barista, Josh, who I used to babysit, is running back and forth from the ovens to the hand-off plane, and has the time to wave at me and smile. He always has a way to maintain his cool. It makes him perfect for this job.

Two other baristas, Bella and Makenzie, are tending to the lobby and assisting Josh with food. Becca and Tobey are rushing to satisfy the crowd at two different espresso machines. Becca is totally in her element, eyebrows bunched and tuning out all the noise.

She looks up and finally sees me. She mouths, "In a hurry?"

"Yes," I emphasize with eyes wide and eyebrows to my hairline. She gives me a thumbs-up, and I know that means I can escape the line. I highly recommend making friends at places of business. Makes life much easier when you're in a hurry. The single-mom card has lost its perks over the years.

"I don't think I've ever seen you here when you're not in a hurry," Becca remarks as she rinses milk pitchers.

"Felicia, I'm always in a hurry!" I wipe the sweat off my forehead. "I woke up late after going back to bed."

"I wish I could wake up late." She shrugs. "The curse of being a barista."

Less than a minute goes by, and Becca has my caramel macchiato hot and ready.

"Oh my goodness, bless you, my child." I take the cup from her gratefully.

Becca gives me a mock salute. "Farewell, Jedi."

I'm about to take a sip of my liquid sunshine and make my crappy morning glorious, but in that same instant the Honey Bucket of a morning continues.

A kid bumps into me.

The lid pops off my cup.

Coffee splatters on the counter. My chest and chin are burning hot.

All I can do is freeze. I have to accept that I now have coffee on my clothes, on my chin, and on the floor.

Becca pauses mid-order and covers her mouth. "Oh no!" She finishes making the drink in her hands before moving to help me. "I'm so sorry, Felicia!"

"I can't go home and change!" I whine loudly. "I gotta get to work!"

Stupid kids. Use protection, people.

"Hey."

I turn and my eyes meet the most beautiful man I've ever seen. Lively, glacial-blue eyes, borderline ethereal. Bald except for his neatly groomed brown beard, long-sleeved shirt clinging to a pair of thick biceps, and jeans that meet down to a pair of black work boots. He gazes at me with genuine care and concern.

"Yes?" I growl in irritation.

"What drink did you get?"

His voice is a bundle of deep, gruff, and comfort all balled up in one. But I'm still annoyed with my life. "Caramel macchiato. Why?"

"I know you're in a hurry, and I haven't touched my coffee," he assures me. "Like, I haven't had a sip. So, do you wanna take mine so you can go? I can just order another one."

Say what now?

"Oh, I don't want you to feel like you have to—"

"I don't." He tries to hand me his cup. "I swear I haven't had a drink. I have nowhere to be anytime soon, and I can see you do, so take mine. It's no trouble at all."

I'm still trying to process that I have coffee on my shirt and that I've made a mess. Having this godsend of a man swoop in and save me is making my brain tweak out just a little. I have to look at Becca, who's watching the whole thing as she cleans the floor, just to make sure that I'm not the only one imagining this. The way her eyes widen, she seems intrigued with his outward kindness.

"Wow, that's awfully nice of you." I'm truly in awe that this person is this kind. "If it's really no trouble—"

"Not at all. Trust me."

I take his drink. No *one* comes to my rescue. Yet, this man is making this huge gesture because he could tell I was in a hurry. Why has mankind not learned anything from him?

"Thank you. Thank you so much!" I could hug him. I could kiss him. I'm sure it would be a make-out session to blow away any woman, but it's not meant to be.

I run toward the door. I want to stay and chat and see if he'll ask for my number, but I'm running really late now. "Thank you!" I wave as I open the door. "Keep up the good work!"

I have no clue why I said that. I'm just grateful that I can finally fuel up for my job. When I take a sip and I don't spill it, I revel in the taste.

To the inventor of coffee, I thank thee.

Chapter 4

Nichole

Okay. I just finished cleaning a ceiling with food stuck on it at a client's house, and it took an hour just to clean her kitchen alone. She left me a plate of cookies as a thank-you gift, though, so I can't complain too much.

But I'm in no mood to cook after that fiasco, which means another boxed meal is what's for dinner tonight. Camilla hasn't given me any spare food, I did mac and cheese again a few days ago, and Kaden isn't a spaghetti person. Maybe pasta and alfredo sauce will do.

Now I'm at the grocery store at Landing Plaza, perusing the pasta aisle, practically slumped over my cart. Grocery shopping is the last thing I like to do after work. Wine and a bath are where it's at.

I look up and see boxes of Hamburger Helper marked half off. Like the angels decided to shine a beacon on it. Now *that* is a single mother's dream come true.

I reach as high as I can to grab the box, but my sore arms and shoulders scream at me. I'm too short to get it myself. I'm too tired for this crap.

I look to my left. Then to my right. No helpers. No taller customers. All I hear is elevator music.

I guess I have to be creative.

I move some products around on the bottom shelf with the toe of my shoe, then step onto it.

Good. Great. That's gained me some height.

I stretch as high as I can, since the box I want is pushed back just out of my reach. I grip another shelf with my other hand to avoid falling over and try again. Yes! I got it.

But I feel myself going backward. The falling part is fun until I land straight on my butt. Good thing I have a cushioned booty.

Then, it gets worse.

The shelf falls toward me, boxes of pasta and glass jars scattering to the floor. I yell and push back to avoid being assaulted by the shelf, and just let myself be covered in sauce. Definitely not the most graceful fall of my life.

Great. Now I'm the helpless pasta woman. I'll just lie here and embrace it.

"Man, aren't you accident-prone."

I roll my head to the side and find a beautiful man at the end of the aisle smiling wide at me.

Wait. I had the same thought the last time I saw him. Bald and bearded with a dark long-sleeved shirt and fitted jeans on strong legs.

Oh God. The guy I met a few days ago at Caffeinated Vino, where I spilled coffee all over myself. Now, I've got sauce all over myself. In front of the same guy.

This couldn't get any worse.

Just like I do in every situation, I laugh. I laugh hysterically because that's how ridiculously embarrassing this is. It's better than crying.

"Cleanup on aisle seven," a monotone man's voice comes over the intercom.

Great. Someone saw the whole thing go down. Just wonderful.

"Here." He moves toward me, making sure not to step on any boxes or broken glass or slip on spilled sauce. I can feel the wetness on my back and arms, and stuck in my hair. Not embarrassing at all.

Once he's standing above me, he holds a hand out for me to grab. The scent of his charcoal and woodsy cologne makes him even sexier.

Steady thy heart.

Finally, a store clerk appears to help. It only took a week for an employee to come by.

"My bad," I say through a fit of hysterical chuckles. "I got a little excited with all the boxed options." Then add with way too much enthusiasm, like I'm getting pumped for a football game, "Boxed dinners are my jam!"

The hot guy snorts a laugh. The store clerk looks at me like I'm a human Wookiee, then mumbles something about getting a mop before walking away.

"Nice cover, Magnum," Hot Man comments.

My cheeks are so hot, I'm glad my dark skin makes it hard for him to notice. "Thanks, I guess," I say with deep shame.

"All jokes aside, are you okay?"

My muscles finally relax enough to feel comfortable looking up at him, now in such close proximity. Those ice-blue eyes are clear enough to cut into my soul, and something about it doesn't make me uncomfortable at all.

"Yeah, by some miracle."

I examine the messy ground and wipe off my pants. "My son loves Hamburger Helper. This store was just evil and put it in a place I couldn't reach."

He cracks a smile. "Out to get you, are they?"

Flirty and beautiful? It's the complete package with a big bow on top. I may have had a hard day, but his coyness is comforting. I scoff playfully. "Well, of course!"

He motions for me to get out of the aisle when a couple clerks show up with cleaning supplies and a mop. Where were these guys when I couldn't reach the freaking pasta?

"How old is your son?" Hot Man asks as I follow him back to his cart with the Hamburger Helper idea flying out the window.

"He's ten." I roll my eyes. "Who's at home playing *Fortnite* without a clue that I'm trying to get him a fancy, homemade dinner."

Hot Man motions to his cart. "Well, based on the contents of my cart, he and I are about the same age."

A pack of frozen burritos. A bag of pizza rolls. A gallon of ice cream. Three TV dinners. "Lord have mercy," I reply. "Have you heard of cooking?"

He gapes in mock outrage. "Says the woman who was about to get Hamburger Helper."

I narrow my eyes at him with a lopsided smile. "I have an excuse. If I wasn't so tired, I'd make fried rice or broccoli cheese soup." I stick a finger at him. "Homemade!"

He lays a humble hand on his chest. "Pardon my manners. Those both sound delicious, though." He peers down at my empty hands. "Sorry, I don't want to stop you from keeping your son alive."

I wave a hand at the aisle behind me. "I'll just do a frozen meatloaf or something." I find myself blushing and focusing on my feet. I don't want to stop talking to him. None of the guys I've dated made me feel this comfortable, free, and made me forget my life for just a few minutes. And so unashamed of my clumsy self.

No. I can't fall for his charming ways. His humor. His ability to put me at ease. His overt kindness. His beaming smile that could wake the dead. "Anyway, thanks for helping me."

I turn to walk away toward the frozen aisle, but I hear him step toward my retreating back.

"You know." I turn to him just before he moves to touch my arm. "While you're here shopping for the fanciest food for your son, maybe you can help me get things for my next meal. You sound like you know some things about broccoli cheddar soup and fried rice?"

I tap my lips with my finger, intrigued, trying hard not to smile. He's making it really difficult for me to pass him up. I could use a night of fun. "Okay. What are you making?"

"I don't know." Then adds in a low voice, "Maybe you could help me pick something? You made me realize a TV dinner isn't gonna be satisfactory."

This man is going to be the death of me if him simply talking makes my entire body hum.

"Hmm." I try to think of what I feel a typical man would like. Whenever I was on a date, the guy would order a burger and fries, or fried chicken, or, well, pasta. "Do you like steak?"

"Am I a man?"

Boy, are you ever. "And potatoes?"

"Who doesn't?"

I smile and gesture for him to follow me.

We're about to enter the produce aisle when he sticks his hand out. "I'm Pete, by the way."

I only shake his hand to be polite, not because I'm falling for his kindness. Not at all. "I'm Nichole."

"Nichole," he repeats with a soft smile. "Okay, Nichole, show me your cooking expertise."

After about ten minutes, I pick out a nice sirloin steak with a small bag of Yukon gold potatoes and a bagged salad. I settle for buying a frozen meatloaf and a bag of veggies to steam. Gotta give the kid veggies somehow. And all I have to do is turn on the oven. Kaden will live.

Pete follows me to a checkout line, patiently waiting as the clerk rings me up. I'm about to pull out my debit card when his hand rests on mine. My heart races and my cheeks heat.

"I got you," he says.

Am I about to save money because he's paying for my groceries? Yes. But I still pull out my kindness card. "Oh no, you don't have to—"

"It's fine." He fishes out his card from his BB-8 wallet. "It's the least I can do. You helped me figure out what to make for dinner."

I'm holding back squeals as I bounce excitedly on my feet. "Hold the phone!" I point. "You have a *Star Wars* wallet?"

He responds with a low chuckle, "I'm kind of a die-hard fan."

I could hyperventilate. He's too good to be true. "Me too!" I barely contain my excitement when my hands flail about. "I have a whole collection of Grogus at home!"

"You'll have to see my collection." He presses his card against the payment terminal. "It'll blow you away."

Is he inviting me to his house to look at his *Star Wars* memorabilia? Does he want to see me again? It's enough to make my heart race and there are hearts in my eyes, but I need to tamp it down.

I'm proud to be the breadwinner, but not so proud I won't let a hot man buy dinner for my kid and me.

"You're so kind," I say genuinely. "Thank you so much."

"It's no trouble at all." The clerk finishes ringing up Pete's groceries, he pays, then retrieves his bags. "I'll walk you to your car."

The few seconds it takes to get to my car, I'm reeling from today's events. Pete is . . . nice. Overly nice. Nicer than anyone I've met in the last year. He's got to be up to something, because there's literally no other reason for him to treat me like a princess.

Not that I'm complaining.

I'm just about to thank him for everything again, but his phone rings. He groans when he sees who it is.

"Sorry, I have to get this," he says, his lips in a tight line. "Maybe I'll see you here again sometime?"

I smile sheepishly. "You may."

"Good night, Nichole."

All he has to do is say my name for me to whimper. "Good night, Pete."

When he answers his phone, I can't help but check him out and get one last whiff of his scent that makes me imagine him chopping wood in a forest. Hot, hot, *hotness*.

That's the problem, though. It's usually the hot guys who are the players. They're the ones who are overly nice because they want some goods in return.

Do not trust a man named Pete, my brain yells at me with flashing alarms. *Don't let him near your goods. You've dealt with enough.*

However, I can still admire him from afar. I'm still a woman. I admire Pedro Pascal from afar because he's an untouchable celebrity. Pete is my Pedro Pascal.

I get in my car and text the girls the events of the last half hour. I'm pleasantly surprised with how eventful this afternoon turned out to be, and it was all good stuff.

Taryn: I believe that's called a sugar daddy, and I think he enjoyed being yours.

Becca: If that's not a sign that he was totally flirting with you, I don't know what is. The coffee incident was just the beginning.

I had a feeling they would say that. I so badly want to believe them and jump on board with whatever chemistry is happening. But I also feel it's necessary to believe that he's this nice to everyone, or he's biding his time so he can show his ugly side, like they all do.

I need to not think about him anymore. I'm determined to focus on being Kaden's mom, and that's what I'm going to do.

Me: I want to believe you guys, but guys do that because they want something. I can't trust someone like that.

Becca: You can't assume that about all men, Felicia.

Taryn: You know next to nothing about this guy. For all we know you'll never see him again!

Me: I know he's a Greek god in human form.

Becca: We need to get you a man, STAT.

I don't know him. I may never see him again. That will help me keep my guard up.

Even if I secretly wanted to take his shirt home so I could smell it whenever I want.

Chapter 5

Pete

I don't know what came over me.

I had a hard day; I only wanted to get a few things at the store to help me survive for the next couple days. I went in with a plan to buy whatever I want and not care about my health in the least bit. I live alone, no one can tell me what I can't eat. Pizza rolls are my Kryptonite.

And, as of a few minutes ago, so is Nichole. By some miracle, I've run into her twice now.

It shouldn't have been so funny, but seeing her on the floor surrounded with boxed pasta dinners, so defeated but amused, was the best thing I'd seen all day. I might be a douche for saying it, but it's the truth.

Helping her to her feet, adding humor to take her mind off the embarrassment, asking her to help me shop just to spend more time with her, all of it felt natural. So natural that it was borderline scary.

I'm an idiot. I never got her number.

My phone vibrating in my hand reminds me why asking for Nichole's number wouldn't have been a good idea.

"Hey, Danny," I answer as I put groceries in the back seat. "What's going on?"

"Hey, Pete. I wish I was calling with good news."

He never calls with good news. He's a lawyer, for God's sake. "Okay?"

"We haven't gotten a trial date for you yet," he explains. "The courts are so busy, you might have to wait till next year."

Next year. It already feels like this debacle has been dragging for a year.

"The only option you have is going back to mediation to figure out a compromise."

I sigh harshly. "We've already done all that."

"I know. And since her name is on the house too, she's just biding her time till you give in. So, my suggestion is to let her have it so you can avoid an expensive court trial and just be free of her."

Anna. The thorn in my side.

"I'm sorry, man. But I'm not letting her get anything." Why should she get her way if she's the one that chose to walk away?

"Well, that's not all."

Oh boy.

"She's threatening to sue if you don't agree."

That news would throw anyone into a panic attack. More lawyer fees.

But I don't panic. I *laugh.*

Not only because she's stooped to this level and it's pathetic, but she doesn't even have the money to sue. I'm sure not giving her anything. Her sugar daddy is broker than a joke. He faked being a rich man when he met Anna, only for her to find out he lived in his parents' basement.

"Are you kidding me?" I say through laughter.

"I know. I would take that with a grain of salt. She has no leg to stand on here."

It's a losing battle for her either way. Seeing her suffer is petty, but man, does it feel good.

Once I finally regain my composure, I say, "Sorry, I'm not backing down. She's gonna have to live with the fact that her pushover ex-husband is no longer a pushover."

"If you want to drag this out, you can," Danny replies in a somewhat defeated tone. "But in my experience, women are pretty stubborn with this kind of thing. Unless there's a compromise that can get you both what you want and put this whole thing to rest."

God, I would love to get her off my back. I'd love to go for weeks on end without her calling me to prove that she's not backing down either. I'd love it if she wasn't such an angry, ruthless woman looking for payback. If all she wants is a compromise, maybe I can make that happen. All I know is, this isn't the same Anna I met all those years ago.

"I can put her and her hobo boyfriend in a nicer apartment," I offer, grasping at straws for a solution, "but that's as far as I'll go. I just want her to leave me alone."

Danny sighs. "I get it. She's a lot to take."

He has no idea. The last few years have been proof of that.

"I'll relay the message."

"Thanks, Danny."

I hate that I created this impasse. It's delaying the inevitable. I have something to prove to myself, and I don't care how long it takes to get the point across. This is the opportunity to grow a spine and stand up for myself. To reclaim my self-respect. There's nothing I want to do less than give in to a woman that had an insane shoe collection that could put Prada to shame.

I pull into my driveway and stare blankly at what was once my parents' house: modern, geometric, and a mix of black and gray. I lean back on the headrest and sigh. I love this house. It's where all the memories of my parents live. Dad didn't want Mom to be alone if something were to happen to him, and refused to let anyone outside the family buy it, so he gave it to me and Anna, and arranged for Mom to live with Kacey and her family. It's not just a house; it's everything my family represents.

I don't know what I'm going to do. This lawyer is costing me about as much as this house is worth. I could use that extra money for Comic Con tickets and cosplay materials. I need to live my geeky life in style.

One day at a time, I guess.

After a few minutes, I muster up the motivation to get out of the car and bring my groceries inside. Once I lay the bags on the kitchen island, I decide to phone the closest friend I have: my younger sister, Kacey.

Kids are screaming in the background when she answers. "Lucas, stop throwing your food! You're not a monkey!"

I pour myself some scotch and pull out a cast-iron pan. "Am I interrupting dinner?"

"No, just a normal Wednesday night with two demons while Kirk's working late *again*." She lets out a laugh that reflects her being on the brink of insanity. "What's up? You have an update on the Antichrist?"

That's her nickname for Anna. There's no better description of her.

I stab some holes into a potato. "Danny called and says he can't get me a trial till next year." I place the potato in the microwave and turn on the stove. "She's threatening to sue if I don't give in."

Kacey first replies with a boisterous, mocking laugh, then asks, "Are you for real?"

"It's fine, Kace. She doesn't even have money to sue."

"No," she replies indignantly. "No. This is ridiculous. Just give her what she wants, numbnuts! This back-and-forth crap isn't worth it! It's not like you don't have options. I told you you can live with me till you find a new place." She groans again. "Hang on." She doesn't even cover the speaker when she shouts at her daughter, "Lottie, get your finger out of the dog's butt! That's disgusting!"

Charlotte gets a little too curious. Most of the time, she likes to explore things that involve germs and everything imaginable that's gross. Like a cat's litter box. Kacey even found her scrounging through a full dumpster once.

"Have you forgotten that this was our parents' house?" I seat myself at the kitchen island. "I can't just give up the biggest gift they ever gave us, despite how they felt about Anna."

"And Mom is living with us and my kids have vocal cords. Sometimes you accept your fate." Her voice gets as stern and deep as Darth Vader when she says, "As should you."

"I'm not letting her win. She doesn't deserve it." I eye the door in the expansive, clean main living room that leads to the garage. "There's so much I can't let go."

"I know," she replies with compassion, "but maybe it's time to decide whether this battle is worth fighting. She wasn't there for you when Daddy died, and never went with you when we had dinner every year on his anniversary. That tells you the kind of person she is. I know you well enough to know you don't want her in your life any more than she wants to be in yours."

Every year, my sister, her kids, and I get together with Mom on the day Dad died and have dinner that consists of his favorite foods: mac and cheese, buffalo wings, and chocolate cake. Anna felt that these dinners were just a way of living in the past—that it didn't accomplish anything. Plus, Kacey's kids annoyed her. Honestly, having her there would've sucked the reminiscence out of the occasion.

"I know," I reply softly. "I'm just waiting for her to blink."

"Ugh, you're such a typical man. But I get it." A pause while the clamor of pots and pans takes up all the audio. "I still want to punch her in the baby maker."

I throw my head back and laugh. A firecracker, she is. "I love you, sis."

"I love you, boo!" she exclaims. "Oh, Mom wants to talk to you. Now, if you'll excuse me, this mommy's overdue for some wine."

Kacey hands the phone over to Mom. "Hey, Petey." She pauses. "First off, what's a baby maker?"

Of all the questions she could ask, she chose that one. "Not answering that. Moving on."

"Okay, fine." Another pause. "What's that noise?"

I turn to the stove and find my steak smoking like a wildfire. I hastily get up, knocking over the barstool in the process, and reach for a spatula. "I'm making a steak and a potato," I answer as I attempt to flip the steak with one hand.

"Wait. You're cooking?"

"I am."

"What's the occasion?" She turns on her warning voice. "I hope you're not cooking for a lady friend. You're not single yet."

Thanks for the reminder, Mom. "No, I'm doing it for myself."

She hums in approval. "Would you look at that? My son's a new man. Now that that whore is gone—"

I snort. Sherri Daley, my unfiltered mother. No doubt where my sister learned it from. "Mom, really?"

"Oh, who are we kidding? We should've had NASA send her to space in a rocket with the aliens."

"Wow. Can you elaborate on that a little more?"

"You're a boob. I live with my grandkids. All they give me is imaginative ideas." She sighs. "Just . . . don't lose yourself in this whole thing, okay?"

It's my turn to sigh. Understandably, Mom worries. Also understandably, I can see what she means. But I know Anna. She doesn't like prolonged tension. "I've explained this. I'm trying to stand up for myself. Dad would have wanted that for me."

"He would also want you to be happy," she argues.

I scoff. "I *am* happy. I'm a bachelor. Maybe I can actually start healing."

"Maybe you can pick up where you left off on that project you were working on with him?" she suggests.

Not the first time she's mentioned that. "Maybe."

"Well, you've got plenty of time now." The kids scream again in the background, and I can hear Kacey yelling at them to knock it off, and it makes me chuckle. "Ugh. I should help your sister with the kids. Kisses!"

I chuckle. "Bye, Mom."

I hang up and move my steak onto a plate, only to find that I burned it on one side. And I cooked it till it was well-done. *Well* well-done.

Steak well-done is a disgrace. I may as well be eating chicken.

Eating through my mediocre potato and disgraceful steak, I ruminate over Kacey's and Mom's words. I'm slowly realizing it's possible to want two separate outcomes equally with every fiber of your being. Anna wasn't there when I needed her most; she ditched me. Of course I want nothing to do with her. On the other hand, there's something thrilling and victorious when you make the other person mad by withholding the one thing they want.

Dad would be proud of me.

"A happy wife isn't always a happy life when she's the ball to your chain," he told me one time while working in the garage. "If she has no reason to not respect you, you have to give her one. And don't stop trying."

I didn't live up to those words when we were together. So I'm doing it now. It's not something I feel like Mom or Kacey would understand.

Maybe you can pick up where you left off on that project you were working on with him.

The project we had barely started on when he died.

I put my plate in the sink and head to the door leading to the garage. I have to pause before opening it. I haven't spent much time in there in the last few years. Mainly because it makes me miss him and his random moments to drop words of wisdom on me. Plus, I'm nowhere near as talented as he was.

The proof is all over the shelves and the work table in the garage when I turn on the bright white light. It smells of cigars and shaved wood—exactly like Dad. Wooden dioramas with 3D carvings of reenacted scenes from movies, books, and video games, all with backgrounds thoroughly painted with the finest detail. Even when he was up in years, he was brilliant. They were all so unique that if you walked into a house that had a wooden 3D diorama, it was for sure done by Sam Daley. Some he sold; some he kept for himself if he really liked it, which was *a lot*. Whatever skills I acquired, it was definitely from him.

The Millenium Falcon. The tree from the opening credits in *Bridgerton*. Han Solo frozen in carbonite. Westley and Buttercup from *The Princess Bride* kissing. Link from *The Legend of Zelda* about to lift the Master Sword from the Pedestal of Time. I helped him with a lot of these.

Then there's the woodworking table. He always sat on the left, and I sat across from him getting paint and superglue everywhere. Right in the middle are three slabs of wood with sawdust scattered all over the surface. I don't know what he planned on doing with that one. It feels so wrong to pick up where he left off without him, working on a project that he had in mind that I know nothing about. Seems presumptuous to touch it.

So there it's been. For five years straight.

The better part of those years where I spent a lot of time grieving and needing my wife's support. When I finally felt myself again, she was off hooking up with someone she felt was "more balanced."

I examine the partially made box and shake my head. I'm leaving that one alone.

But there's one thing I will do that cheers me up.

On a rusted metal shelf by the door, I reach for a warped cardboard box and pull off the lid to find a stacked pile of cigars. I'm not much of a smoker. When I did smoke, it was always cigars, and it was always with Dad.

I use the lighter sitting next to the box and take a few puffs. I turn on an old Bluetooth speaker covered in sawdust and paint spatters and plug in my phone. A song I listened to with Dad all the time comes on, one that I'm sure was made in the sixties, but one that always made us feel good. One that never fails to make things better when I listen to it.

As I puff my cigar, I let myself remember that feeling, and sink into it.

Chapter 6

Nichole

Camilla and I went on a run this morning. Surprisingly, the weather was mild and it wasn't raining. She isn't usually awake, but she had woken up early and couldn't go back to sleep, so she texted me and we went for a five-mile run. I told her about Pete and the grocery store incident.

"I think you can delete that Beeline app," she had said with a knowing smile. "The man is an *ángel*."

"I'm cautiously optimistic," I had replied. She and my friends seem to believe Pete is going to be the game changer, and they haven't met him. Maybe that's a sign?

Once we get home, I have half an hour to get Kaden out of bed. Perfect timing to get myself cleaned up.

Everything after the shower was a hot mess. I'm going to need another one already, because I'm sweating yet again. Kaden was hesitant to get out of bed to say the least.

I guess it's my fault. I introduced Kaden to *Fortnite* and he's been playing every chance he gets. Especially in the mornings when he's supposed to be getting ready for school. Why oh why did I introduce him to video games?

That's right. Because I want to be an awesome mom and I love my child.

As soon as I drop off Kaden at school, I head to my only client of the day. Jane owns six cats and her house smells like she sprayed air freshener full of cat piss. I go in with a mask every time because the smell is so pungent. I lovingly call her Cat Piss Jane.

Thankfully, when I do leave her house every time, it smells more like the cleaning aisle at the grocery store. I don't care that the chemicals burn my eyes and nostrils; I just hate the smell. Becca has one cat, and that's enough for me to handle. Six is an illegal animal shelter.

Camilla calls me as I drive to Cat Piss Jane's house, while I mentally prepare myself to gag when I arrive. "Hey, Camilla."

"Hola, Nee-cole," she greets me with a cheerfulness that I don't have after this morning's run. "Listen, I was wondering if you had room in your schedule for another client."

"Today?" *Please oh please let it be today.* Now, *preferably.*

"Yes," she says. "His name is Pete Daley. He got my number from one of my clients in Bellevue. He says he's hoping to find someone to clean his house today before an important client meeting, and also continue coming every week."

Pete Daley . . . Can it be that guy . . .?

No. That's too much of a coincidence. Creekside has hundreds of people; there has to be more than one Pete in this place. And he wants me to come every single week? Who is he, Emperor Palpatine?

She giggles. "He says he's a bachelor and he's terrible at cleaning up after himself."

Crap, I think it's him.

"He asked if I could clean his house in the next hour or so, but I am booked back-to-back with clients today. He seemed desperate. Can you take him on?"

Oh darn. That means I have to call Jane and rearrange my schedule. I'm sooooo disappointed. "How big is his house?"

"It's about five thousand square feet."

My eyes bulge out of my head. "That boy be crazy! That's gonna take me all day!"

Camilla laughs. "No no, he just needs the kitchen, living room, and dining room cleaned," she clarifies, much to my relief. "However, if I were to pick anyone to clean a bachelor's house, it would be you. You're the GOAT. Is that the right term? Goat?"

I snort. There's something to be said about a sweet Mexican woman using the lingo of Gen Z.

If this is the godlike Pete that I met at the store five days ago, then I have to decline. I *cannot* be in the same room as him. I'd scrub the same table ten times because I would just stare. And, for some reason, I'm a hot mess every single time we've been together. All of two times, but that's two too many.

On the other side of the coin, this is an opportunity that just happened to fall in my lap. I need the money for Kaden's plane ticket, and I need more work in order to pay for that. I have to take this.

"Yeah. Sure. I can do it. Just let me call my client and let her know I need to reschedule. I'll just tell her I had a family emergency."

"Gracias, *gracias*, chica!" she exclaims. "I'll text you his address."

Great. A new address. That I'll need directions to. GPS won't help because I still manage to get lost. Then I sweat and curse and scream at the fact that I can't find the street names that the GPS claims are there and I swear it's lying to me.

I already know I'm going to be late arriving at this guy's house.

I'm a half hour late to Pete's house.

One thing that worked out this morning is that Jane was willing to push her house cleaning to later in the day so I can fit Pete into my schedule. I should be elated, but I'm stressed out and sweaty, and I haven't even moved. The only plus here is I managed to hold back from using foul language.

I turn on streets that end in "place" when I'm supposed to turn on streets ending in "street." It all looks the same, and Siri changes the route with every turn I make. I want to choke her. Creekside has three neighborhoods, one of which is for people that have money, which is where I'm lost. It's not a big neighborhood, so why is finding his house so freaking hard?!

I park in the paved driveway in front of a two-car garage. The two-story house is largely square with natural stone siding and wood textures, and so many windows looking out onto the lake. A balcony on the second floor wraps around the house with Adirondack furniture.

So, this is where Pete lives. He's clearly well-off if he has a gorgeous house like this. It's practically a mansion.

And I'm about to clean it.

I'm suddenly nervous. Not because I'm late, but because I look like I did a workout and I'm sure I've got BO. My *Star Wars* bandana is already damp. This is an extremely nice neighborhood, just up the hill from Lake Washington and walking distance from the Seattle Seahawks football training center. The houses here are worth millions of dollars, they get a three-hundred-sixty-degree view of the water, and are updated with the latest and greatest style and technology. I'm an Ewok with tangled hair in comparison.

I adjust the rearview mirror to check my face and hair to make sure nothing is amiss. I shouldn't have done that, though, because I find a whole new problem.

I have a pimple. Right in the middle of my forehead.

That is so attractive. Said no one ever.

My phone pings.

Becca: I really wish it was legal to punch customers in the throat. Someone lost her mind because her iced tea wasn't sweetened like she claimed she asked for when she really didn't. #facepalm

Oh good. Someone else who's riding the struggle bus.

Just to make sure she doesn't feel alone, I take a picture of my face, emphasizing my new pimple like I won a prize. I send it with my text.

Me: Well I just arrived at a brand-new client's house, and I have a freaking pimple. It might as well be a beacon for a lost ship. It's been a stressful morning and I haven't had coffee yet!

Taryn: Can you stop by my office so I can pop that thing?

Wow. Skipping right to the pimple.

Becca: No, I wanna pop it.

Taryn: I'm still healing from that crappy interview and my coworker yelled at me for not saving enough coffee for her. I should pop it.

Becca: Felicia Nichole, can you grow a new pimple so we both have one to pop?

Me: You guys are disgusting.

Becca: I love you too.

Me: Listen Felicias, this client's name is Pete . . . What are the odds this is the same guy I met at Caffeinated Vino AND the store??

Becca: That would be cute and freaky.

Taryn: Then you're in for a world of trouble. Need some ice to cool those burning loins?

Becca: Great. I'm dying laughing in the middle of work and my coworkers are giving me strange looks.

I finally find the strength to get out of the car. I still have to haul my bucket, mop, chemicals, and vacuum up the two flights of steps to the front door, which is sure to induce more sweat. Showering this morning was counterproductive.

It feels like it takes me an hour to reach his porch with all my crap. Even the door is beautiful. Polished wood, an old-fashioned iron door knocker nailed on the top like it came from medieval times, and a small window above it. I feel so exposed.

The door opens. Just as I suspected, it's Hot Man Pete. My stomach falls to my butt and my heart launches into flutters. Is it possible to be disappointed and excited all at the same time? Because not once has he seen me in a stable state of mind.

"Well, hi!" he exclaims, surprised as I am that I'm standing on his porch. His spotless, smooth-as-a-porpoise porch.

"H-hilo," I spit out. Dear God, I already sound like an idiot. He's so beautiful it makes me insanely stupid. "Sorry, that was a mix of 'hello' and 'hi.'"

Annnndddd my butt is sweating.

He laughs and points a finger at me as if he's trying to remember something. "Nichole, right?"

I chuckle nervously, using my shirt to wipe the sweat off my forehead and hide the pimple. I'm flattered he remembers my name. "Yeah."

"Hang on. If you're looking to clean the pasta aisle, you're very much in the wrong place. But I won't say no if you're here to clean my house."

I snort and hang my head. I wasn't at the time, but now I'm amused by the fact that he witnessed the mess I made on myself. On aisle seven, to be exact.

"One of these days when we have a random meetup, I'm not gonna be such a disaster."

Pete's lips rise. "I'd be lying if I said it wasn't entertaining."

"Anyway, I'm so, so sorry I'm late. My son took a little longer than normal to get ready for school, then I got lost finding your place, and I haven't even had my coffee—"

"No coffee yet?" Pete gasps and feigns shock with his hands to his cheeks. I love that that's the one part he paid attention to. "That's unacceptable." He opens the door wider to make room for me. "Come in. I'll make you some."

"Oh wow, that's so nice of you—"

To my surprise, he grabs my bucket and mop and carries it inside. "It's no trouble at all. A morning without coffee is a morning sure to be pure garbage."

His living room sits on the left immediately upon entering, ivory carpeting with a cream-colored L-shaped couch, and glass end tables that shine with the light from the windows. The entryway is a polished black tile that runs from the front door to the kitchen straight ahead. A spiral staircase leads to the second-floor landing where I see a bathroom in the middle of the hallway. Vaulted ceilings make this place seem three times bigger. Everything is so modern and chic; the kitchen has a solid granite island, gray countertops, and black cupboards. I'm secretly wishing this was my house.

He's a bachelor, and he lives *here*?

As I step farther into the house, I find myself so stinking happy, I can barely contain myself.

Shelves in his living room are full of *Star Wars* memorabilia, including two Stormtrooper costumes in full display in the corner next to a big screen TV. *Star Wars* action figures line the hearth above the fireplace.

He wasn't lying. He really is a hardcore fan.

All the shelves and tables could use a good wipe down and dusting. I only have a few seconds to revel in the fact that I have the honor of doing it, but I have to get a move on if he's having an important business meeting. I'm definitely not going to be the reason his house isn't in order.

Something occurs to me, and I should've asked the moment Pete opened the door. "Did you know I was a house cleaner?"

He shakes his head with a look of surprise. "Not at all. A friend of mine is one of Camilla's clients, so I called her hoping she could do a last-minute cleaning. She told me she was sending someone else and that she would do an excellent job." He winks. "Didn't think it was you, but I look forward to seeing you live up to your reputation."

"No pressure or anything." I examine the space around me to get an idea of what needs to be done. "Listen, I know you're on a time crunch, so I can get started in the kitchen—"

"Shhh." Pete holds a finger to his lips. "You've had a rough morning. Let me make you coffee at least. You can't start a day without some. It's almost a sin not to."

He leads me to his impeccable kitchen. The sink is full of dishes, crumbs litter the counters, and I have to control my urge to twitch at the mess.

He moves to turn on his silver espresso machine that I'm sure cost thousands of dollars. His positive energy is so contagious, and it's exactly what I need. "What was it that you like to drink? Caramel macchiato?"

My jaw drops. "You remembered?"

"Hard to forget when you see someone spill it on themselves and they just happen to also love caramel macchiatos. Not to brag, but I make coffee as good as that place." He winks again. "Anything you want, I can make."

My heart stops racing and my muscles loosen. "Well then, a caramel macchiato, please."

I've watched Becca make me this drink numerous times, but watching Pete do it so smoothly and casually is so much more mesmerizing. Maybe because he has a coffee shop on his countertop? I don't know, but it's all so fascinating.

He grinds the espresso and puts it in the portafilter, twists it into the machine's group head, and lets it work its magic.

"So," he starts as he moves the steam wand away from the machine and pours milk into the pitcher. "Have you always lived in Creekside?"

I shake my head. "No. I'm originally from Detroit."

He proceeds to steam the milk, and it's a screaming, paper-tearing noise that fills the entire kitchen. "I'm originally from Kansas, but I've lived here since I was seven years old. This actually was my parents' house till about five years ago."

That explains it. "It's absolutely stunning."

He winks again. "I agree."

God, this guy could melt my clothes right off with those eyes. And I wouldn't mind.

He takes a mug and pumps syrup into it from a stand that holds a plethora of flavors. He taps the pitcher on the counter to level out the foam, then pours it into the cup, then the shots straight down the middle. Then to my favorite part: the caramel in a perfect crosshatch. It floats on top of the foam like a puffy cloud.

"Here you go." Pete hands me the mug with the work of an artist. "A caramel macchiato."

He leans back against the sink and watches me with folded arms and a playful smile. I feel his eyes on me as I examine the perfectly steamed foam and the caramel drizzle. It's so beautiful, I almost feel bad for drinking it.

I meet his gaze. "Why are you looking at me like that?"

"I have a feeling you take your coffee seriously." He shrugs. "And I just called myself a fantastic barista. It would be embarrassing if you thought differently."

The corner of my mouth lifts. "Again, no pressure."

He laughs as I take a sip.

It's silky. It's smooth. The caramel is a brown buttery sweetness mixed with the milk, and the bitterness of the espresso makes a perfect balance.

Sorry, Becca, but this takes the cake.

"This is amazing!"

Pete seems surprised as he lifts his eyebrows. "Really?"

"Oh my goodness!" I take another sip. "Caffeinated Vino doesn't even compare. This is exceptional. How did you learn to make such amazing coffee?"

"Exceptional? I'm honored." He puts the milk pitcher in the sink. "My sister was a barista. When I started working from home more, I got an espresso machine so I didn't have to keep spending money on coffee whenever I go to Seattle. She would come over and show me recipes and how to use this giant contraption." He gives the machine a couple pats. "Best investment I ever made."

"Why were you in Caffeinated Vino that day, then?"

He shrugs. "I had to go into the office and I was too lazy to make my own coffee." His smile hitches. "I'm glad I went because I got to help a woman in distress."

"This woman in distress appreciates you coming to my rescue." I take a few gulps from the mug before I ask, "What else do you make with it? Do you have a favorite drink?"

I never expected my day to go like this. To show up late to a new client's house, to a guy I've met before—twice now—only for him to serve me coffee and talk to me like I'm a friend, and make me feel comfortable. I don't remember the last time I felt so relaxed and at ease.

"I experiment with everything," he answers. "I keep things simple. Sometimes I'm good with straight espresso with a couple packets of raw sugar."

I gag at the idea of plain black coffee. "I can't drink coffee straight. It's so gross."

Pete chuckles. "When you're desperate, you don't care all that much."

I don't even feel stressed anymore. He managed to calm me down with homemade coffee and casual conversation. The man's a genius.

I gulp down the rest of my drink. "Well, I should get started on cleaning. Your client will probably be here soon."

Pete looks at the Apple Watch on his wrist. "Shoot, you're right. Here, let me show you what needs to be done, and where I keep my cleaning stuff if you need it. I can make you another macchiato if you want so you can drink as you go."

I smile so wide it hurts. "I would love that."

There are three bedrooms upstairs at the end of the hall. The master bedroom hosts the best view of the lake. Yet, Pete decides to do his work on the kitchen island. It makes me wonder if he's going to be watching me so he can critique my work, like most clients do. Not like I haven't done this for twelve years or anything.

But hey, he's letting me drink coffee as I scrub the counter of a half bathroom, even if it's gone stone-cold. I can't complain. Even so, he sits on a barstool in front of a laptop. Doing that all day must be a nightmare for his back and neck.

Once I'm done with the bathroom, I move into the second living room on the other side of the kitchen, and I feel like I'm entering a new planet.

He has bookshelves upon bookshelves of *Star Wars* collections. The big, important, valuable things. Not to mention the most expensive things one could possibly imagine.

A Darth Vader helmet, a Darth Maul mask, a black series snowspeeder, a LEGO set of Darth Maul versus Ahsoka, and—

A LEGO Millenium Falcon.

My dream collectible.

This all has to be worth thousands of dollars. Money I don't have if one of these breaks. I don't know Pete very well, but he's not incapable of suing me if I damage something. A nervous sweat breaks out all over my skin.

I very carefully lift each item to dust under it. My sweaty fingers slip all over the items and leave ugly streaks. I don't even bother touching the Millenium Falcon. Heck, I don't even dust that area. His business client won't notice. I'm on a time crunch anyway.

I move over to the main living room with the Stormtrooper costumes. I feel like I'm giving the enemy a pat down, something that, in a *Star Wars* universe, I would likely get from one of these guys. Those menacing eyes from those helmets literally glare at me as I run a cloth over their shoulders.

"You should be cleaning *me* off, traitor," I mumble at it as quietly as possible.

I feel its eyes burning in the back of my head as I return to the kitchen to warn Pete that I'm going to run the vacuum. By the time I'm done, I'm sweating even more. Vacuuming is its own workout.

"I'm done," I announce.

Pete lifts his head and lowers his laptop. "Thank you so much for coming on such short notice."

"Glad I could help."

I watch as he stretches his back and arms, rolling his neck back and forth. "Why do you work down here and not in the office?" A workaround question to see if he's been watching me clean the whole time.

He chuckles lightly. "The answer sounds ridiculously lazy."

I lean against the doorway between the kitchen and dining room with a side smile. "Which is why you should tell me."

His chuckle grows a little louder, but he shyly aims his gaze at the countertop, and it's the most adorable, shameful look

I've ever seen. "It's closer to the fridge when I'm hungry," he explains, "my espresso machine is down here, and the lighting is so much better than my office upstairs."

"The only 'lazy' part I got from your explanation is that it's close to your fridge."

He holds out his hands and shrugs. "Hey, what can I say? I'm a guy."

I laugh as I wrap the cord around the vacuum. I don't want to leave. He's the only client that has made me feel as comfortable as I am now. Everything I was feeling when I first met him at the coffee shop is all the same. The biggest perk is his *Star Wars* fandom.

"I was literally sweating, cleaning your *Star Wars* stuff."

"Why?" he asks through a laugh.

"I was afraid of breaking it!" I exclaim. "I literally have no water left in my body. I'm just sweating coffee now."

He raises his palm. "Listen, the last thing I want you to feel every time you come over is stress. So next time you come to clean, I'll just take the stuff off for you, and you won't have to worry about it."

"Oh no, don't! I love *Star Wars*, remember?" I point to my bandana. "This is just a hint of the Grogu collection that keeps growing in the corner of my bedroom."

"Grogu?" He rears back as if this is a turnoff. "Grogu isn't enough proof. Most people collect Grogu things because he's cute."

Fair point. Then I remember something that has me searching frantically through the photos in my phone. I show him the one I'm looking for. "I dressed as Leia and my best friend Becca dressed as Rey at a baseball game last summer for *Star Wars* fireworks night."

He nods at the photo, impressed. "You played off Leia really well, especially with the wig."

"Amazon, I'm tellin' ya." I put my phone back in my pocket. "Have you always been a *Star Wars* fan?"

"Since I was a kid." He pulls out his own phone and scrolls through what looks like Emerald City Comic Con photos. He pulls up a picture of a man in brownish clothing with a brown cloak, his fingers like tiny, open-ended tubes, eyes as huge as baseballs with a purple glow, and green, rubbery skin. The best representation of an alien. "I dressed as a Rodian last year. I was so freaking hot in that costume."

"Well, yeah!" With all the clothing, the mask that is most likely not breathable, and the gloves that are made like alien hands, it doesn't surprise me. "I was there last year too!"

"You were?" he exclaims. "Who did you dress as?"

I giggle. Not the Santa-Joker giggle I had when I was on that date with Trevor, but a genuinely throaty chuckle that's seductive and flirtatious. "I was Ahsoka one day, then Captain Marvel the next."

He leans forward, totally shocked in a way that makes me grin. "You were Ahsoka?"

"Oh yeah. I have the whole getup. I also did a photo op with John Boyega."

"So did I!" He raises his hand for a high five. "Did we just become best friends?"

I laugh at the reference and nod. "Yep!"

Pete looks at his watch and my stomach drops. Our *Star Wars* conversation has to end. “Crap. My client will be here any minute.”

I rush to the living room to pack up my stuff, and I feel him examining my work behind me. “Everything is sparkling. It looks really good. Will you be available next week?”

I immediately stop what I’m doing and try not to smile. “You want me to come back?”

He shrugs. “Yeah, why not? You’re a great cleaner.” His arm spans the space around us. “I know the place is huge, and you probably have other clients, so what if you cleaned the downstairs one week, and the upstairs the next, and just alternate? That way it’s not too much all at once.”

I don’t care how many clients I have. I don’t care that I’m insanely attracted to him. I will fit him in any day. I can look, but I’ll never touch. Even if he’s being awfully sweet and considerate of my schedule.

I’m not an animal. I have self-control. I’ll just keep telling myself that.

“Yeah. Just text me your schedule. We can work something out.”

He fetches his wallet in his back pocket. “Listen, because this was so last minute, let me give you a well-deserved tip.”

My instinct tells me to reject his offer because he’s so kind. But I really, really need the money. “That’s sweet of you, thank you.”

He peers down at his feet, twisting his body back and forth like he’s mustering up courage for something. “If you’d like, maybe we can grab coffee sometime.” His eyes meet mine, and his smile is so adorable and sweet. "You know, when you're not stressed out and wearing coffee on your shirt."

My cheeks heat and I avert my gaze. A man I'm very strongly drawn to is asking me out. I have no logical reason to turn him down. The chemistry and banter are more natural than natural peanut butter. It's a living dream.

That's the problem.

No. I'm no one special to him. If it's not me, he'll find someone else. I'm just a convenient single woman, and he's only going to be this charming until we go out on a date where I find out he's wearing a bald cap and secretly a sex offender. Men aren't honest anymore. Plain and simple.

My hand reaches for my chest. "I'm so flattered, Pete. I'd love to grab coffee with you . . . but I can't."

His full eyebrows snap together. "Oh. All right. Can I ask why?"

Probably the politest way to accept a rejection I've ever seen.

How do I explain this without making him crazy? I mean, he already knows *I'm* crazy. I just don't want to make it worse by pouring out my life story to someone I barely know. "I've had some seriously bad luck with men this year. I think I need to focus on my son for the time being."

Pete folds his arms, plumping up his pecs, and nods. "I get that."

He may as well have punched me in the boobs. Rejecting him *sucks*. "I'm sorry."

He vehemently shakes his head. "Please don't apologize. You're being a good mom, and I totally respect that."

I hold back my bashful smile. “Thanks.”

We hear the sound of a car door closing outside when he hands me the wad of cash, and I know my time is up. At least he wants to see me again.

“I’ll text you.” Pete clears his throat as he walks me to the front door. “Thank you so much again.”

By the time I get to my car, I don’t even want to go to Cat Piss Jane’s house. I just want to run everything with Pete through my mind and figure out where I could’ve changed the scenario. The fact that he’s sweet, attractive, and charming makes it even better. He didn’t brag about his money or try to make out with me. He was a true gentleman. Even so, I stuck to my guns.

Holy crap, that was hard to do.

Even so, I have to remember what I decided. I can’t trust men. Not anymore. This is exactly how they are on the surface, then they turn out to be the most awful humans in person. I can’t keep falling and turning in the same cycle over and over again.

I’m Kaden’s mom, and that’s all. Doesn’t mean I can’t admire Pete in my mind, though.

I pull out my phone and send a text, all while emitting a loud groan.

Me: You guys, my new client happens to be the guy I met at the store. And he loves Star Wars! Probably more than I do.

Becca: I think this is called fate. I mean, what are the odds of this happening?

Me: I know. I'm insanely attracted to him, but I can't fall for him. I'm so tired of being screwed over. How am I gonna keep being his house cleaner if he's this sexy?

Becca: Hm . . . The client and a house cleaner . . . sounds like a really bad erotic movie.

Taryn: Or some super weird role-playing. Has he asked you to clean his pipes?

For the love of God.

On the way to Jane's house, I reconsider what I said to Pete. I stuck to my guns. I should be proud of myself.

So why does it feel so wrong?

Chapter 7

Pete

When I opened my door this morning, I did not think it would be Nichole—the gorgeous, funny woman I met last week—standing at my doorstep. My heart flopped in my chest, and before I knew it, I was flirting and making her coffee. When a woman is a hardcore *Star Wars* fan with the superpower of cleaning a house on a time crunch, there's no turning down the charm.

I even had the courage to ask her out. I haven't done anything that courageous since Anna. I hid it well, but her rejection surprised me. Although, I do understand it.

Having her as my regular cleaner is going to be dangerous for me. No woman will want the baggage I refuse to throw away, let alone a single mom. It's a natural deterrent. I'm a skunk. A skunk that finds himself craving a spider that happens to be poisonous.

"Oh." Cece, the Caffeinated Vino manager with a nasal voice and erratic blonde hair, moans as she sips the latte I made her. "If you had a coffee cake or a cinnamon roll, I'd die and go to heaven a happy woman."

I wince. "I don't have any, sorry."

"Well, put on your domestic pants and be prepared the next time I come over." She winks and intertwines her bright red manicured fingers around the coffee mug. "I don't even care if it's from Costco. I just think if there's nothing to pair the coffee with, then what's the point of having coffee at all?"

"Besides the fact that it's America's lifeblood?"

"Well, it's mainly Washington's lifeblood." Cece shrugs. "Just sayin'."

Either working with Cece is going to be fun, or it's going to be as exhausting as having my niece and nephew spend the night at my house. I have to provide pastries when she comes over, and she has the desire to draw Creekside into spending money on more coffee.

I clear my throat. "So, what can I help you with, Cece?"

She takes another sip, a milk mustache planting itself on her upper lip that she doesn't even notice. For funsies, I don't point it out to her. "I want to launch some new products. Everyone's on this fad of low sugar, gluten free, vegan, vegetarian, or whatever crap is new to this place that tastes like glazed sawdust." She waves her hand in disgust. "Anywhoodles, as much as it makes me gag, maybe Caffeinated Vino could cater to that kind of crowd. Maybe it could bring in more people. Especially in the evening when the bar opens and everyone wants a nice treat." Her bright red lips spread into a smile. "I was hoping you could help me with some food ideas, and share it on our social media to spread the word for our new launch. Take some photos, videos, yada yada yada."

I take notes on my laptop as she speaks. "That sounds good. When are you hoping to have this done?"

Not that timing would matter much. I'm self-employed and have my own marketing business with my friend Kevin. I can do whatever I want.

Cece shrugs, propping her chin on her hand. "I was thinking sometime in May?"

"That's plenty of time."

"Well, I need pastry ideas that I can refer to my bakers so they can do trial runs with some recipes. So if you can at least have a list within the next week or so, that would be super helpful." She pats my hand. "And make sure they will be reasonably priced."

I hum. "That will take some time to brew."

Her shrill, staccato laugh explodes in my kitchen while I hold back my grin. Dad was the king of puns. Like father, like son.

"You! I like a man with a sense of humor." She drinks the last of her latte. "Okay. I'd love to have you help me with this. Show me what your plan is."

For the next half hour, I draw out a schedule of posts for their social media page, the hashtags I plan on using, and the event page I'll create to give the community time to see and express interest. She left my house with a bright red lip stain on my cheek and erratically clapping hands. It's safe to say she's happy.

Once I get back on my laptop, my phone rings, and my heart starts racing when it reads "Antichrist." It used to just say Anna until Kacey took my phone and changed it.

"Hello, Anna," I say in a monotonous tone.

"Have you talked to Danny yet?" she asks in a smarmy, saccharine voice; it's like horrible feedback on a microphone. She's been calling me with this question at least once a week for the last three months. I'm stupid enough to think that whenever she calls, she has a change of heart and is willing to make amends, or even apologize for the lack of compassion she showed the last few years since Dad died. Each time, she's shown where she stands on us altogether. There's no redemption.

"Yes."

"Then why haven't you taken me up on my offer? Do you really wanna be sued?"

Her attempt at this scare tactic is laughable. "You can't sue me."

"Then give me the house and this all goes away," she whimpers. Why I ever thought that voice was the sexiest in the world is beyond me. "It's a generous offer if you think about it."

"Yeah. Not convinced. Bye, Anna."

"You owe me, Pete!" Her shriek blasts through the speakers on my phone. "All I wanted was some reassurance that you still loved me. Then you leave me stranded with nothing, not even a suitcase!"

The look on her face that day actually has me cackling inside. "You did that to yourself, lady," I retort through laughter. I decided long ago that whenever she calls, I'm going to enjoy it by making fun of her and rubbing her mistakes in her face. Better than sulking in pity.

"Well then, I'll drag this out as long as it takes," she says with scorn.

"You'll cave. I know you too well, Anna."

"When it comes to getting what you deserve, I don't mind waiting. Although, I *am* getting impatient."

"Why? Because you realized that you had it made here?" Her new boyfriend has absolutely nothing to offer her other than a good time. "The house with a view of the lake? Or the master bathroom that *isn't* in my mother's basement?"

She screams in frustration, and I'm enjoying it immensely. "You stopped paying attention to me! I kept trying to tell you how I felt, and you barely listened. You can't blame me for finding someone who made me feel valuable and beautiful again!"

My side of the story is very different. I did my best to let her know I loved her and appreciated her for sticking around. I tried cuddling with her and showing affection, and even thanked her for staying with me. I don't ever recall her trying to tell me that that wasn't enough. I was just expected to figure it out.

I was expected to pick up on nonverbal cues.

"Well, you left when I needed you most. I guess we're even."

I hang up on her while I use up the remaining cackles left in my system. What goes around comes around. I'm done being her doormat. Pete Daley is a new man now. A new, almost-single, thirty-five-year-old man.

When I was growing up, Dad told me to find a woman that always makes your heart beat at full speed, because that's how Mom always made him feel. At one time, that's how I felt with Anna. Everything seemed right when she was around. All I needed was her smile, and my day got easier.

Dad had a bad feeling about her, and I ignored him. In the end, he was right, and I never got the chance to tell him. She didn't know how to not have high expectations of everyone around her. I liked to think I made decisions that would make him proud. Marrying her was not one of them. I have to live with that regret for the rest of my life.

Sitting in a drawer in my kitchen island is a selfie of Anna I used to like having next to my laptop when I worked. Now, she's covered in devil horns, a unibrow, and a mustache, thanks to my sister and her Sharpie. "Good riddance, witch," Dad would say.

Now I can start to move on. I want to move on to Nichole.

Kind of.

Maybe I should have told her I'm still married. *Why* I'm still married. Then it might put the kibosh on our flirting. Which I really, *really* don't want to do. She's by far the most amazing person I've met, just in the short time I've known her. A sweet, hilarious, and fun single mom who works hard and does it all without a faltering smile says a lot about her. We get along so well, we have a lot in common, and her wit and smile get me every single time.

But . . . she said no. However, that doesn't sound like a permanent answer. She *wanted* to go out with me. She's just scared. I understand that. Making the leap to just ask was scary enough for me.

What if she said yes? I'd be a married man having an affair. Sort of. How would I go about telling her that? She's already had bad experiences in dating. Why add to that?

To top it off, she has a son. I never pictured myself being a dad to someone else's child. If the father is still involved, then where would my place be?

Anna didn't want kids at all when we got married, but I assumed she would change her mind eventually, especially once we spent time with my niece and nephew. When she kept telling me that kids are "a constant inconvenience," I just accepted that I may never be a dad, and shoved it to the back of my mind. I just went on with life. I ignored the nagging feeling that maybe I'll never carry on the family name.

If the opportunity presented itself to be a dad, I can't imagine myself rejecting it. For the time being, maybe it's best we don't do anything just yet.

I get back on my laptop and start researching high-selling pastries to get the ball rolling for Cece. Not a lot of choices that are different from other coffee shops.

This is going to take a while.

Chapter 8

Nichole

I've been to Pete's house once. One would think that if I've been there once, I don't need a GPS to find it again, right?

One would be wrong, because I got lost finding his house. Again. With GPS. The only thing that I recalled was what his house looked like from the outside, because I remember thinking it was gorgeous.

Well, I did make it to his house. Eventually. With my palms sweating.

Get it together, Felicia.

Pete texted me and said he left his key under the mat, so I assumed he wasn't going to be home. I let myself in, hauling in all my equipment, only to find that Pete was, indeed, home. Working on the kitchen island, eyes glued to his laptop, three coffee mugs in his workspace, not even acknowledging my presence. He was zoned in, and it was a little freaky.

This may be the bad side I'm seeing.

"Hey, Pete," I say warily.

"Hey," he replies in a rushed tone, not even looking up from the screen.

I step cautiously into the foyer and lightly tread toward him. We may just be professional with each other, but for some odd reason, I feel comfortable enough to ask, "You okay?"

Finally, he looks up, and I can see the stress lining his beautiful face. He sighs heavily. "I'm so sorry. I'm doing research that's not leading me anywhere, and I can't even think straight." He runs his hands over his scalp. "And I've had three cups of coffee."

"It's not even ten in the morning," I voice with concern.

"I know." He groans. "I've been tasked to come up with unique pastries that are gluten free, vegan, vegetarian, all that BS."

I frown. "Well, shoot. Anything I can do to help?"

His smile hitches. "Make time slow down?"

"Ha! I wish that every time my son grows out of his shoes."

Pete flinches as if something just occurred to him. "Wait. How often do you go to Caffeinated Vino?"

"Like, every day." I chuckle. "My friend Becca works there. Sometimes she gets my drinks for a discount."

Pete hums thoughtfully. "If you go there a lot as a customer, maybe you can help me with some pastry ideas. Cece wants to do a launch with the new products by May."

I know nothing about dietary needs like he mentioned. Becca eats gluten free; she'd know more than me. "Is she looking for particular recipes? Like cakes and brownies?"

"She's open to whatever. But that's what makes this so difficult. I can't really find *anything*. I also have to manage their social media to build it up, you know?"

I step farther into the kitchen and lean on the island countertop. "Are you a social media coordinator?"

Pete shrugs. "A glorified one. We focus on marketing with quality photos and creating flyers and such."

I wiggle a thoughtful finger at him. "You know, this could work in your favor. You have free rein to do what you feel is best for the business. She's relying on your experience in this area."

"Yeah, but that's the problem. I know nothing about pastries other than eating them. That's why I'm asking you, as a customer, what would appeal to you?"

Pete wants me to help him with his job. I'm honored that he wants my opinion. But I also have my guard up, because this makes getting closer to him even more possible. I can't let that happen. Need to let him down easy.

"Let me see if I can come up with something," I say while grabbing my bucket and scrubbing brushes. "I'm gonna clean upstairs."

As it turns out, his *Star Wars* fandom expands into the office. Which, to my disappointment, he forgot to take things off the shelves so I don't break out in nervous sweats from dusting. I swear I'm in a museum of George Lucas's ideas wherever I go. Which means I really shouldn't touch any of this. If I can manage to make an entire shelf at the grocery store topple over, I can topple anything.

One of the items catches my attention. A helmet with a bunch of scribbles on it, which I'm guessing are autographs. I seriously don't think this man is missing a single thing in *Star Wars* history.

Yeah, I'm not laying a finger on that. It's too important. I'm honored that he even trusts me to clean the space *around* his stuff. I barely want Kaden to go *near* my Grogus.

With my palms still sweating, I work the dusting cloth on the shelves, around the figurines, and the valuable helmet, taking extra care to make sure the fibers don't get caught on anything. After ten minutes, I've barely finished two of the four shelves. I've spent way too much time here. There's more of this space to clean and I have another client to get to afterward. I need to hurry.

I speed up my dusting to what I'm comfortable with until the cloth sticks to a sliver of protruding wood. My heart races in a panic as I jerk the cloth free and pick off the fibers that the shelf took from me.

Screw this. There're more important things to clean. Moving on.

Another room across from his bedroom is full of exercise equipment. A bench with weight plates, a treadmill, kettlebells, and a rack of free weights. I guess this is how he keeps himself in good shape.

I wipe off the equipment and disinfect the seats and anything that comes in contact with sweaty body parts. The entire time, I picture Pete lifting weights in a tank top and gym shorts, biceps flexing, sweat beading all over his neck and chest, working on those thighs that his jeans show off so well . . .

I need to get out of this room.

It's no better when I go to clean his bedroom. It smells just like his cologne. He has a king-size mattress all to himself, with his bedspread the same colors as the rest of the house and a cushioned headboard. I bet the sheets smell like him too.

Good Lord, woman, just clean the room and be done with it.

After another hour, I'm much more exhausted than normal. Maybe because I'm calming down from being so stressed out. How sad is it that fear of ruining valuable materials stresses me out more than divorcing my ex-husband? Sad. Very sad.

A caramel macchiato would really hit the spot.

Wait. There's an idea. A caramel macchiato-type pastry. Take a coffee drink—or even matcha or tea in general—and turn it into a pastry.

I feel like a genius.

"Did you come up with any ideas?" Pete asks the moment I step in the foyer.

Wow. Really didn't think he'd hold me to it. "Actually, yes."

"Yes!" He claps in relief and sits up straighter on his barstool. "What do you got?"

"You and I both love caramel macchiatos." I hold out my hands. "What if there was a caramel macchiato brownie? Or fudge?"

Pete nods, flexing his arms as he folds them over his chest in a way that accentuates his pecs. *So hot.* "Okay. Keep going."

"Take a coffee drink, like a mocha for example, and make a cake with chocolate and coffee flavoring?" Ideas are nonstop now. "Or lemonade made into a pound cake with strawberry icing. Or matcha and white chocolate chip cookies. Some Earl Greys have lavender, so you could make cupcakes with lavender frosting."

Pete smiles wide. "Those are freaking awesome ideas!" He hurriedly writes in a notebook next to his laptop. "I'll take a look and see if there're any recipes that exist. If not, I'll just come up with a list and Cece's bakers can figure something out." He breathes out heavily in relief, a burden sliding off his chest. I did that. Me, of all people. "You have no idea how much that helps. Thank you so much!"

He leaps up from the stool and hugs me. My entire body goes rigid, surprised at this sudden reaction. The moment my senses are assaulted with mahogany, charcoal, and cedar, I melt into his embrace and hug him back. His strong arms make me feel safe. Protected. Like he would never let anything hurt me.

Yeah. This was a bad idea.

I pull away and jam my hands in the pockets of my *Friends* leggings. Pete lets go like I'm on fire and backs away.

"Sorry," he mutters. "Got a little excited."

I wave my hand in dismissal. "All good."

It's really not. My heart is debating whether it needs to beat faster or stop altogether.

"I should get going," I say, pointing to the front door.

I collect my things in the foyer. I came here with the expectation that we'd keep our distance and not have a chance for conversation. But he needed my help, and I wasn't going to leave him stranded.

I still don't want to leave. That's the one part that lingers. Plus, I want to talk about his collection.

I really should leave. I really, *really* should.

I tell my brain to screw itself when I walk back into the kitchen. "I wanted to ask, what's that helmet you have with all those autographs?"

Pete flashes an impish smile. "That, my lady, is my most prized possession. A clone helmet from the 332nd Division autographed by the voice actors from *The Clone Wars*."

My jaw goes slack. "I'm so glad I didn't ruin it, then."

He palms his face. "Shoot. I forgot to take all that stuff down." He looks at me apologetically. "I'm so sorry. I've had so much going on, I forgot you were even cleaning the upstairs today."

I wince humorously. "I guess I don't feel bad for telling you that your shelves didn't get a thorough dusting."

He shakes his head and laughs, the tension seeping out of him. "Do you ever not wreck things or worry about wrecking things?"

I double over in a self-deprecating laugh, then straighten up and shift to a serious expression. "No."

Pete chuckles a little harder as he fumbles with his back pocket. "Are you heading out?"

I let out a harsh breath. "Yeah. I have one more client today."

He pulls out his wallet. I can't believe how many bills he has in there. I wish I could fumble through that kind of money like I'm not insanely rich. I need that money, but maybe I should play innocent.

"Oh, you can just Venmo me for today."

"I will, but I want to tip you too." He slaps two fifty-dollar bills on the kitchen island and slides them to me. "You have been a huge lifesaver. I have no time to keep up with the place anymore, and this project is going to be a time suck, so having someone do it and be completely amazing at it has been more helpful than you know."

I can't help my own impish smile that tugs at my lips. Part of me feels bad for taking his money, since he's being so sweet and generous. On the flip side, I'll be able to book Kaden's flight well in advance. "Thank you so much."

I wait for him to pull it back the moment I reach for it. Or for him to make a joke about my circumstances that completely destroys my self-worth. Or gives me a stack of his work simply because he doesn't want to do it.

None of that happens.

I take it, and he winks at me with a small smile. He's such typical romance-novel boyfriend material.

If it's too good to be true, it probably is.

If I've learned anything of value from my mother, it was that tidbit.

I repeated that tidbit to myself the rest of the day. It helped to some extent, except when I cook dinner later that night for my friends and kids, and my brain wants to remember when I helped Pete shop for dinner two weeks ago. Something as simple as grocery shopping turned out to be fun, just because I was doing it with him. I should just do all of my grocery runs like that.

Keep dreaming, sister.

Taryn checks her phone as I search for cooking materials in the kitchen. "Yay! Kitten just used the litter box!"

"You get notifications on your phone when your cat takes a poop?" I ask.

"At least I know she's healthy!"

"She's not mentally healthy," Becca retorts. "She's the demon spawn of Satan."

Taryn gasps. "She is not! Look." She shows Becca her phone screen. "Look how she's walking. You just hurt her feelings. That's why she don't like you."

"One minute she's rubbing up on me, then two seconds later she hisses at me and bites my hand!" Becca shrugs. "She's the devil's cat."

"Felicia, tell her she's wrong," Taryn demands of me.

"Are you serious?" I shake my head. "I woke up with her sitting right in front of me, then she whacked me in the face when I moved then ran off!"

Becca motions to me. "See? Proving my point."

"She knows y'all talk smack about her," Taryn says under her breath.

"Can one of you help with these potatoes?" I ask.

Becca's the first one to leap from her seat. The best cook of the three of us. "I got you, boo."

Kaden and Oscar emerge from Kaden's bedroom to sit at the dining room table with Taryn. Good, the perfect time to change the subject from Taryn's bipolar cat. "How was school, baby?"

Taryn props her chin on her hand and inclines her head, giving Kaden the pressure to give a good answer. I throw some frozen chicken tenders on a sheet pan and preheat the oven. Becca helps by cutting potatoes and mixing a bagged salad.

"Good." Typical kid answer.

"There's going to be a science fair in May," Oscar fills in. "It has to be a project related to something we've learned during the school year."

I shove the chicken to one side of the pan to make room for Becca's oiled and salted potatoes. Good thing she loves to cook; I don't know what I would do without her help. Or Camilla's leftovers.

"Have you learned anything that you can use for the project?" Becca inquires from the kitchen.

"No," Kaden says through a laugh. "School just started!"

"Maybe you can study the bad effects of a middle-aged woman drinking too much whiskey," Taryn suggests as she downs a shot. Such a wholesome example for my child.

I point an oven-mitted hand to Taryn while eyeing my son. "Don't do that." I set the oven timer. "You'll come up with something, kiddo. You're smart. Let me know what you decide so I can get the stuff for it. And it can't be related to *Fortnite*."

"Aw man. Okay. Can I play *Fortnite*?" he asks with a cheesy smile on his face.

"Only if you do the dishes after dinner."

"I'll happily be a test subject for your project if it'll help you, as long as it doesn't involve needles," Taryn tells him. "Or feet." She shivers.

"Oh, me too!" Becca raises her hand.

"Fine. Just come up with something that can give legit results, and I'll get the supplies for it." *Now that Pete seems to be giving me extra money for no reason*, I say to myself.

During dinner, Becca waves her fork in Kaden's direction. "I know you said the project can't be related to *Fortnite*, but what if you tested the effects of excessive video games or something?"

"That would be fun!" Kaden exclaims.

"Oh please, you would never get anything done," I say.

"My alcohol idea still stands," Taryn interjects, her fork pointed at the boys. "Might teach y'all a lesson about what to expect."

"I don't think the school would like that," Becca replies.

"No, they would not," I concur.

"I don't know what else I want to do." Kaden frowns.

Poor kid. He has no father figure to guide him in any one direction. Something as small as a freaking science project has me doubting my ability to be both mom *and* dad. If Jared had stuck around instead of finding interest in another woman, I wouldn't have to be both.

I reach across the table and pat his hand. "You'll figure something out, baby. No matter what it is, we got you." My Felicias nod. "And, no matter what you choose, it's going to be fun. Okay?"

His mouth tilts in a smile, then he continues eating his chicken.

Maybe I really *can* play both roles.

My alarm must hate me, because it doesn't go off, even though I swear I set it last night.

But, no.

I should've been awake an hour ago to take Kaden to school. I'm shocked he didn't wake me up himself. Which, on its own, is concerning. He always milks the alarm for a few minutes before getting out of bed, but never for *this* long.

I kick off the covers with the ferocity of a karate black belt and bolt to Kaden's bedroom. Maybe by some miracle he was responsible enough to ask Camilla for a ride to school. In that case, I'd be proud.

But, also no.

He's still sleeping. Fantastic. I'll have to take him to school super late.

I move his body back and forth by the shoulder. "Kaden, wake up."

It's completely dark with the fan on his desk to serve as white noise to keep him asleep. The star stickers that glow on the ceiling provide a measly amount of light, and a lava lamp that very dimly illuminates *The Lego Movie* posters on the walls. I stumble over his toys on the floor to reach the curtains at the window and throw them open. Still gloomy outside and it brings no light into the room. Why did I think that would work?

"You're late for school," I say over my shoulder. "Like, super late."

"I don't feel good," he mumbles into his pillow.

"Hm." That might explain why he's still in bed, but he's also done this before to avoid school. I don't fall for it that easily. The last time he faked being sick, I came home to him prepared to jump from the second floor of the fourplex onto an old mattress. "Let me feel your head."

He rolls onto his back and I lay a hand against his skin. It feels warm, but I chalk it up to him being under the covers. Not enough evidence.

I go into the hall closet and pull out the thermometer.

"Aw, man." He groans when I bring it to his room.

"Just be thankful I'm not putting this in your butt." I shove the thermometer in his mouth and let the numbers tick higher and higher. "Don't take this out till it beeps."

I go back to my room and fetch my phone. No better place to complain about my troubles than with my Felicias.

Me: Pray for me. I'm super late, and Kaden says he's sick, but I'm not sure he is.

Becca: Has he done this before?

Me: Remember the mattress incident?

Becca: Oh boy. Well, whenever I tried to get out of going somewhere by faking being sick, my mom always felt the glands of my throat to see if they were swollen. If they were, that was the first sign I was actually sick. Try that with Kaden. Like where the jaw meets the neck.

Me: Hold on.

"Mom, it's beeping!"

I go back to his room to take the thermometer out of his mouth. “Let me check your throat.”

He knows I hardly ever do this, so he gives me a strange, suspicious look. “Okay?”

Lo and behold, his glands are swollen, and he has a one-hundred-degree fever.

“Craaaaaap,” I whisper to myself when I go to the kitchen in search of cold medicine and text Becca.

Me: He really is sick. Thank you for giving me a technique to use from now on.

Becca: You got this, Felicia. I believe in you.

Most of my family is either over on the peninsula or back in Detroit. No one can watch and take care of him but me. I have to make quick work of texting my clients to reschedule with them. Including Pete. That thought deflates my very soul. Like Anakin burning to death.

It takes me a few minutes to fetch Kaden water and orange juice, then I come in with his archnemesis: Nyquil.

“No no no no! I hate Nyquil!” He rolls over to use the pillow as a face cover.

“Believe me, I hate it too, but I need you well so I can go to work and pay to keep you alive.” I scoff and roll my eyes at myself. “Why am I explaining this to you? Take your medicine!”

“No,” he draws out.

I blow out a frustrated breath. He doesn’t like being sick and rejects the one thing that will help. “Just take half a cap’s worth, sip some orange juice to get the taste out of your mouth, and you can hate me the rest of the day. Deal?"

"No."

I set the Nyquil cap on his desk. "Okay. You asked for it."

I pick up my disobedient child and flip him onto his back, then reach for the Nyquil on his desk. He kicks and thrashes so much that the cap knocks over and ends up on his pajamas, his sheets, and his face.

"Ew, I can smell it!" he shrieks.

"You wouldn't have to if you just *swallowed* it!"

"It's disgusting!"

"Why are you testing my patience, child?"

He twists his body to hide his face from me. I can't believe this is how my day is going to begin. I pour more Nyquil into the cap on his desk and prepare to win this battle.

I climb onto the bed, sit on his shins, and hold his arms down.

"Who are you, The Rock?" he shouts. "How are you so strong?"

"I don't run marathons for nothin', boy!"

I snatch the cap and hold it over his mouth. His incessant whining is like unoiled gears on a bike. He still resists, silly boy that he is, but he's become too tired to continue fighting with the way his body slowly relents. "I can do this all day, Kaden." I really can't. Bluffing is my last resort.

Finally—*finally*—he lifts his head and I drain the cap in his mouth.

"There you go." I gently clap his cheek a couple times. "Good boy. That wasn't so hard, was it?"

"Whatever," he complains as he rolls back over on his Nyquil-stained sheets. For someone who hates the smell of Nyquil, he sure doesn't mind sleeping in the mess. He really must feel like crap.

I chuckle as I leave his room, and that's when I realize that the wrestle with my son took a lot out of me. Good thing he didn't call my bluff. I would've been in for a god-awful day.

I make it back to the kitchen, partially sweating, where I left my phone. I have a flurry of reactions to my cancellation.

Paula: Aw, poor thing! I hope your baby feels better!

Grace: No worries at all! I'll see you next week.

Greta: I have to admit, I'm a little annoyed by this last-minute cancellation. I really needed my windows cleaned today. Maybe you should plan your appointments better next time.

Of course Greta says that. She's a bitter old woman with a Saint Bernard that constantly drools all over anything and everything, and she literally refuses to pick up after herself because she assumes I'll just come and do it for her. I'm very much okay with having a break from her.

I'm also very much okay deleting her text and moving on to texting my girls.

Me: So I had to cancel all my appointments, including the one with Pete, which really sucks. To top it off, I just had a Nyquil battle with Kaden. He thought getting it all over his sheets was better than just taking the freaking medicine.

Becca: Why so disappointed about Pete? I thought you didn't want to trust him or anyone. Wink wink nudge nudge.

Taryn: I think it's because our Felicia won't admit that she likes someone who could actually be a quality man.

I hang my head. I can't be convinced that's true. That just leaves room for me to get my hopes up and be disappointed again.

Bringing the walls back up.

Me: Nope. I can't like him. He's too good to be true.

Taryn: Denial denial denial . . .

Becca: Sure. Whatever you say.

Leave it to my Felicias to deny my statements. *True* statements, I might add.

Pete: That really sucks about your son, Nichole. Do you need anything?

Speak of the devil.

And he's the only client who has ever offered something remotely close to assistance. Like, ever. However, only someone who's looking to get into my pants would be this generous and kind . . . and so downright sexy.

Not helping.

He's not actually going to do anything. He's just being polite. No one is that willing to help.

Me: What I would really love is for someone to hold my child down when I give him his next dose of meds.

Pete: I hope you're not asking me to do it. That's a surefire way to get a child to hate me.

He's not wrong. If anything ever happens with me and Pete, I'd hate for Kaden's first memory of him to be traumatic.

Pete: Maybe you can send me your address so I can order some things to be delivered to you, if you're comfortable with that.

If you're comfortable with that. I must be tightly wound up because him being considerate is downright hot.

And who am I to say no?

I give him my full name and address without hesitation, then go about cleaning my own house.

Chapter 9

Nichole

Funny thing about cleaning houses for a living: You never want to clean your own home on your days off. I did it today because, you know, I'm tethered to a sick kid. The gray clouds outside make the opportunity perfect too.

By midafternoon, I've made my living room sparkle and my kitchen counters are clear except for the dish rack full of clean dishes. Oh, and Kaden's been asleep for hours. I have to pat my productive self on the back.

I also end up getting a text from Becca asking to come over for a bottle of Kim Crawford and to watch *Friends*. Not even my snotting child could stop her from coming, plopping on my couch, and pouring herself a glass.

"Dang, girl, did you have a bad day?" I ask after she shoots down the wine. "It's three in the afternoon!"

"It's five o'clock somewhere." She pours herself more. "My manager drives me nuts sometimes. She told me to 'find a way to work faster,' as if that helps speed things along."

"Oh really? Constant nagging doesn't make you work better?" I motion to the bottle on the side table next to her. "Actually, I'll have a glass of that too. It's been a day."

Becca hands it to me. A woman after my own heart. I don't hesitate to take a big gulp straight from the bottle. "I still have to wash the Nyquil out of Kaden's sheets."

She hangs her head and silently laughs. "Okay, you win."

I down another gulp, then plop on the couch next to her. "Heck yeah, I do."

She gives me a mischievous grin. "So . . . Did you talk to Pete today?"

I smack my lips after another sip of wine. "He asked if he could do anything, then asked if he could send me some groceries."

Becca excitedly slaps my arm. "He so likes you."

"But I'm afraid I'm misinterpreting it. Like, maybe he's like that with everyone." I release a heavy sigh. "I just don't know if I should wait to be excited or if I should just let myself feel whatever I want to feel."

She gives me a knowing grin. "You know, I was thinking . . . What are the odds that someone comes along the moment you decide you're done with men? It's like God was like 'hold my beer' and *bam*!" She claps. "There was Pete."

I scoff. "Oh, Felicia, if only I had that kind of luck. I think God stopped answering my calls a while ago."

Becca slaps my arm again. "Oh stop. He'll answer you." Her lips form a tight line. "Jared, on the other hand . . ."

I clap in reminder. "Which reminds me! I'm getting close to having enough money for Kaden's plane ticket!"

"I'm happy for you, but I'm still annoyed that you had to pay for it to begin with." She shakes her head. "Why didn't you just tell him where he can shove it?"

I wanted to do more than that. I wanted to include some choice words and some well-thought-out insults. But I had to put things in perspective. Not for Jared's sake at all, but for my child who is aggravating when he won't take his medicine when he's sick.

"He still needs his dad. Even if he's a man whore. And he really loves Kaden."

Becca hums and sips more wine. "I guess," she pretends to relent. "You're a good mama."

"I know." I wink. "What about you? Have you heard from Shawn?"

She blows a raspberry. "Not since the last time he messaged a couple weeks ago." She wiggles a finger at me, pretending to be serious. "But there's some old retired men that have potential. One guy called me 'hot rod' the other day." She flaps her arms in an exasperated way. "I don't even know what that means."

As a barista, Becca has a chance to meet everyone who lives around Creekside and hear the neighborhood's gossip. Which means she gets firsthand details on who's single and who just got out of a relationship, so she looks out for potential dates for me. They're all duds, though, because they end up so not being my type physically.

I chuckle and shove at her shoulder. "There you go! Grab yourself an old man!"

Becca makes a gagging sound and gets up from the sofa to get water from the kitchen. "Maybe when I lose all self-respect." She sighs, wistfully staring at her glass for a moment. "I wish I had what you have with Pete."

"Nothing is even happening with me and Pete."

"But he likes you. And—" She holds up a finger to stop me from arguing. "—you like him. Don't even deny it."

I try to hide my elated smile, but it breaks through. "Yeah, I do," I answer breathlessly. "I really do."

"Ha, I knew it."

I throw my head back and groan. "I can't help it. He makes it so hard not to. But it doesn't mean anything will happen."

"Let's face it, Felicia. You'll cave," she argues. I examine her face and the reason behind her somber tone as she sits back down on the couch. "I miss that feeling when you know you like each other. Or just the beginning of a relationship when you're the happiest you'll ever be." She sips her water. "I genuinely am happy for you that you found a quality man. It's just hard for me 'cause I want that too."

I grab her hand and squeeze it. "You'll find that too, Becks. Look how long it's taking me." My calling her Becks should tell her how sincere I'm being.

She gives me a look that says she doesn't disagree. "I guess what I'm most afraid of is once you find the one and get married . . . you'll ditch us. Forget about our weekly Felicia meetups. I worry about that happening with Taryn too." She shrugs. "All my friends in the past did that."

"I think Taryn is determined to be single forever. You don't have to worry about losing her." I chuckle.

"I have more hope for her than I do myself. She'll get snatched up soon." Her face twists in worry. "I don't know. I feel like I'm selfish for feeling this way."

A part of me is surprised to hear this. I know Becca wants a relationship, but I never realized that she was afraid of losing her friends. I guess I can understand where she's coming from. But even though she's scared and a little jealous, she's glad I'm happy. She just wants to be *happier* for me than she is.

I reach for her knee. "Listen to me, Felicia. Your friends in the past that ditched you after getting married? They weren't your real friends. You have real friendships with me and Taryn. I knew that the moment we sat in this apartment when it was empty, drinking and talking for hours, that we formed something special." I lean in a little closer, squeezing her knee. "I promise you, if I ever get married—"

"You will," Becca interrupts firmly.

"*If* I get married again," I reiterate, "I'm *not* going to forget about you. Whoever I end up with is going to have to deal with the fact that you guys are the most important people in my life. I may want to spend a lot of time with him, but nothing else will change with the three of us. I promise."

Becca purses her lips, then reluctantly nods. "Okay."

We lean in and give each other a hug. Becca embraces me tightly, sniffling quietly.

"No, no crying." I grab the bottle of Kim Crawford from the table behind her, repeating her words from a few weeks ago. "We drink, *then* we cry."

She cackles as I pour her another glass, wiping the tears away with her sleeve. "I think it's dangerous that I've almost drank this whole bottle and it's not even dinnertime."

"It's companion drinking. It's an acceptable practice."

"Oh, is that what we're calling it?"

"Now we are."

There's a knock at the door. I rear back in surprise as Becca shoots me a confused glance.

"Were you expecting a package?" she asks.

Oh shoot. Pete. "Pete may have had groceries delivered. I totally forgot."

Becca gasps. "I have the privilege of seeing how well he knows you?" She erratically claps. "Oh, this is good."

Oh man. This is going to be interesting.

Chapter 10

Pete

This is by far the boldest thing I've ever done.

Screw the fact that I'm still legally married. If a woman I like needs help and is in distress, what sort of man would I be if I didn't jump to her rescue?

Not a very good one. Not one who really, really likes Nichole Tyler.

And I really, *really* like her.

From a moral standpoint, I shouldn't have feelings for her. I shouldn't be here at her door with a bag of groceries in each hand. I really shouldn't have gotten this present for a child I've never met before because I actually care about making him feel better.

The woman has changed me, and I've only just met her.

I knock on the door. There's some mumbling that I can't decipher, then a dark blonde woman of short stature who is definitely not Nichole opens the door. I start to panic that I'm at the wrong unit. Maybe this is her roommate that she never mentioned having?

"Hi, is there a Nichole Tyler that lives here?" I try to peek over the woman's head to find her.

"Well, yes," she answers coyly, leaning against the doorway with an inquiring stance. "And who might you be?"

A woman is blowing out a nervous breath somewhere in the background, and I'm pretty sure it's Nichole.

"I'm Pete. I'm one of her clients. She told me Kaden was sick, so I thought I'd drop by with some essentials."

The blonde friend's jaw is on the floor and she twists to look behind her, shifting her weight. "Well well well," she coos. "Someone is special enough to get a personal delivery."

Finally, my dream woman comes up from behind her friend, her face frozen in surprise.

"Hi," she croaks.

I smile brilliantly. God, she's adorable. "Hey."

She shakes her head and moves to open the door wider. "Right. Come in, come in."

I set the bags on the table. The variety of colored marks on the wood are clear signs that she has a child. A child that loves to have fun and be creative. "I know I said I was gonna have things delivered to you, but I didn't want the delivery person to give you crap products or pick the wrong stuff and not have you be able to return it. So, I made sure to get good ones. And—" I fumble through a bag. "—you told me Kaden loves *Fortnite*, and I found this while I was at the store."

I pull out a box and show her a dual pack of *Fortnite* themed Nerf guns.

"Oh my gosh." Nichole takes the box and turns it over in her hands, mouth gaping in what I hope is awe. Otherwise, I made a huge mistake giving a kid a weapon. Her dark, beaming eyes that match her all-white smile settle the debacle for me.

"He would love this!" She holds up a hand. "Hang on. Let me go get him."

My sudden unease of that idea moves me to grab hold of her forearm. My fingertips tingle at the smoothness of her skin. Not nearly as much as when I gave her an impromptu hug for her help. Holding her for just those few seconds is a measure of comfort I haven't had in months. Maybe years.

This isn't all that different, with Nichole's eyes shining with delight and . . . desire? A fight within herself that I selfishly wish she would just give up.

I suddenly remember why I'm holding her arm—nervous about meeting her son for the first time—and I drop it like a piping-hot cast-iron pan. "I don't want you to feel like you have to wake him up—"

"No, no, it's okay!" Her voice is suddenly high-pitched and shrill. Even her friend flinches. "He'll be so happy!"

Nichole gives the box back to me and races down the hall, leaving me alone with her friend. "I'm Becca," she says to break the silence. "Feel free to call me Becks."

I hold out my hand. "Nice to meet you."

Becca's eyebrows raise as we shake. "You too." She brings her hands to her hips. "You're a brave one. You delivered groceries yourself, you're meeting one of Nichole's closest friends, *and* her son."

"Why brave? Is he scary?"

Becca blows a raspberry. "Nah, he's a good kid. He's actually quite chill. What you really have to worry about are her best friends." She chuckles and pats my forearm to ease the tension. "I kid, I kid."

The front door swings open out of nowhere, making me and Becca jump. A tan, brunette woman enters and shuts the door like she lives here too. She freezes upon seeing us.

"What am I, chopped liver?" she bellows at Becca. "No one told me there was a gathering in here!" Her eyes find me and she grins. "Oh, hello."

"Taryn, this is Pete," Becca says, her eyes wide with a hidden message that somehow Taryn reads crystal clear.

"Hi, I'm Taryn." She waves at me shyly.

Nichole walks back to the dining room table with a kid stumbling behind her. Same complexion as Nichole, his hair styled in a short afro, wearing a *Transformers* T-shirt and navy-blue sweatpants. His eyes are drooped and blank. Dang. He really must not feel good.

He stops and peers up at me. "Mom, who's that?"

Well, I asked for this scenario. Time to prove to myself I'm cool and can be this kid's friend.

I lean down to Kaden's level with an empathetic smile. "Hey, Kaden. I'm Pete. I'm a friend of your mom's. I heard you were sick and that you like *Fortnite*, so I thought I'd get you this to make you feel better."

I show him the box and Kaden *beams*. He feels horrible, and all it took to breathe some life back into him was a *Fortnite* toy.

He practically snatches the box from my hand. "Wow, this is so cool!" he exclaims through all the congestion, then darts down the hallway like he forgot he was sick thirty seconds ago.

I impressed Nichole's child. Mission accomplished.

"What do you say, bud?" Nichole calls.

"Thank you, sir!" he manages to shout before slamming the door.

I double over in a chuckle and Nichole gives me an apologetic look. "I may have cured him."

She waves a hand. "Oh, he's still sick. The excitement will last a minute and he'll pass out again." She moves to put the groceries in the kitchen. "Oh, those are my besties." She motions to them. "Becca and Taryn."

"We've met," I inform her.

"We're otherwise known as the Felicias," Becca adds.

"'Felicias'?" I repeat and eye Taryn as well. She gives me a shy smile and says nothing. Not much for talking, I see

"It's a long story," Nichole answers. "They live in the units above me."

I smile. I'd love it if Kacey and Kevin could be my neighbors. Life would be fantastic. "Oh, that's nice."

"Yeah, it was mainly out of pity for Nichole since she needed an apartment that we all applied for at the same time," Becca volunteers. "Then we got drunk and became friends. Moral of the story is alcohol is the answer to everything."

Taryn adds nothing to the statement except a shy nod.

"My kind of people," I say through a laugh. "I like it."

Their outward comments amuse me. They would all get along great with my sister. Hopefully, if the future is bright, Nichole can meet her and bring her "Felicias" with her.

I look at my watch. I'm supposed to be on a call with Kevin in an hour. I want to postpone it just to hang out with Nichole, whether her friends are here or not. "Shoot, I need to get back home."

Nichole frowns. Good, she doesn't want me to go either. But she rights herself. "Well, thank you so much for bringing this over!" She books it to the front door as I turn the knob.

"Of course."

I gaze into her brown eyes. Our hands twitch and twist at our sides, each wanting to do something, but unsure of what. I just wait. I don't know what I'm waiting for exactly, though. Maybe for her to say she's changed her mind. Maybe give me a hug that doesn't make her uncomfortable. Or for her to kiss me on the cheek.

That's a stretch. I want her to give in, but I'm going to let her make that call.

We resort to an overwhelmingly disappointing handshake. Her elegant, slender hand grips mine, shyly avoiding my gaze. We stay there and watch the tension implode in front of us.

Seconds tick by, turning this from overwhelmingly disappointing to awakening. She's still holding my hand. By instinct, I run my thumb back and forth over her soft skin. Something so simple is proving to be so electrifying. Her whole body stills, yet she doesn't tear herself away. Nor do I want her to.

She finally meets my eyes. Hers are swimming with desire. At least, that's what it seems like, because I know it's in my eyes too. That one look makes me weak in the knees.

I slowly move my hand from hers and smile knowingly. I know she felt something. "I'll see you ladies later," I announce while keeping my eyes locked on hers. I don't want to leave any more than she wants me to, but I'll stay all day if I don't go now.

Her friends bid me goodbye and I shut the door.

"Chugga chugga yum *yum*, he's cute!" Becca shouts loudly through the door. "Good job, Felicia!"

I have to bite my fist to keep myself from uproariously laughing. I stop and back up, just to hear more commentary.

"Can you at least wait until he's left the parking lot to say stuff like that?" Nichole scolds.

"Have we met?" Taryn adds. "We never wait to add our commentary."

I'm just about to walk away when I hear Becca add, "He's really good at fitting into those jeans."

"Oh my goodness, Felicias, stop!"

I book it back to my car before I explode with laughter. The comments are something else, but I can't say I hate it. I have their approval and we're not even dating. That's good.

One part of my brain is telling me to spare her feelings and leave her alone. The other part is telling me I need to stop letting Anna hold me back from living my life. I'm basically a bachelor. Just not in the legal sense. Something I can accomplish easily if I give her the house.

Everything in my body rejects that idea. Which means I need to keep standing my ground.

God. What am I thinking? Even if Nichole and I were dating, I wouldn't tell her anything right now. She doesn't need to know; it'd be too early for that anyway. All that would achieve is making her life more complicated. I don't want to do that to her. She has a kid.

I'm driving myself nuts.

The cold fall air blowing through my open window doesn't seem to get me to snap out of it either. I need a woman's input on a woman's feelings, and I can only think of one person I can call who understands me and gives advice, even unsolicited.

"What?" Kacey barks sleepily when she picks up. "I hope this is worth interrupting my nap for."

Because I'm such a typical older brother, I decide to mess with her. "I . . . I need help," I say in a tremulous voice. "They're gonna kill me. I'm . . . scared."

The questions come out like a Jedi with a blaster pistol. "What? What's the matter? Are you okay? Do I need to call the cops? Do I need to beat up a hoe?"

I chuckle. "No, but now that you're awake—"

"Oh, I wanna hurt you so bad," she replies with a deathly grumble. "What do you want, slut?"

I let out a belly laugh. "I had to have a little fun. But seriously, I do need help."

"Like with life advice or with carrying another Death Star-related thing that weighs a hundred pounds?"

I roll my eyes. "It was a costume and it wasn't that heavy. I need life advice."

"Hmm. Sounds serious."

"I guess you could say that."

"Well shoot. What is it? Wait, I have an idea." I hear the rustling of sheets. "I'm coming over."

She hangs up and cuts off any chance of argument on my end. She lives five minutes away, but she cuts it in half when she drives her minivan like a starfighter. "I'm a mom. Time is precious," she said the last time I got in the car with her. Too many sudden turns had me rolling all over the place, then she ran over a kid's bicycle that was left on the sidewalk. She kept driving like she didn't notice anything, and I told her I'd never get in the car with her again.

The screech of tires in my driveway two minutes after I enter my house makes me chuckle. Like clockwork. Then she opens the door without knocking.

"I really hope you didn't destroy any more bicycles on the way here," I comment the moment she closes the door. "I won't help you if you get attacked by angry parents again."

She struts into the kitchen with a casual shrug, the total opposite of what her driving skills are like. "I was intrigued and time is precious." She slaps her purse on the island. "Plus, I wanna finish my nap on the guest room bed."

"You'll do anything to sleep on that thing, won't you?"

"Three hundred fifty thread count, long staple supima cotton, and sateen finish?" She sighs contentedly. "It's like sleeping on an orgasm."

I snort and shake my head at her lack of a filter. "You're insane. My house cleaner just changed those sheets, so I don't wanna have her change them again."

Kacey freezes, holding up a hand. "Hold up. House cleaner?" She leans forward like this is a deep, dirty secret. "You hired a maid?"

My shy smile appears of its own volition. "Maybe."

She quirks an eyebrow. "That was a heavy 'maybe.'" She motions to the espresso machine. "Make some coffee."

Leave it to her to not only make herself at home, but also order me around in my own house. I love it.

I take a deep breath when I put coffee beans in the espresso machine. "I sort of have a crush on my cleaning lady."

"Say what now?!" I can't tell if she's angry or excited, especially when she pokes the countertop with her fingernail. "Details. *Pronto.*"

As I grind the beans and get mugs ready, I explain how I hired Nichole to be my house cleaner and we hit it off with coffee and *Star Wars*. Kacey utters the spontaneous "uh-huh" and "yep, yep" between sentence breaks. I debate whether she's urging me to rush through the story or if she's about to blow her lid.

"I had just dropped off groceries and cold medicine for her and her son when I called you," I finish when I hand her a finely crafted latte.

She giggles with a hint of mischief, the mug just barely touching her lips. "Oh man, you've only known her a few weeks and you got it *bad*."

"I know." I groan and slap my face in my palms. "It's torture."

Kacey sets her mug unusually harshly on the counter. "Let me guess. You want to ask her out, but you don't know if you should because she doesn't know you're still married, am I right?"

My mouth curls in distaste at the truth. "Yeah."

"And you don't want to tell her because you know she'll tell you she would rather you be divorced first, right?"

". . . Yeah."

"You also don't wanna burden her with this because she's a single mom and deals with enough."

I sigh with a subtle groan mixed in. Somewhere deep, deep, deep within me knew she would say all of this. "Why do you know everything?"

"Because I'm a woman. That's why you called me."

"Well, can you tell me what to do? 'Cause I have no idea."

Kacey looks at me like I'm too stupid to know the answer on my own. "You know what you need to do, Petey."

Give Anna the house and get the divorce, the one thing that will solve everything yet the one thing I refuse to do. "That's not an option."

"Then you need to leave her alone." My stomach sinks. "You're too stubborn to free yourself of the Antichrist, yet you want to date freely with nothing standing between you. You can't have it both ways, bro." She shrugs. "But I can't tell you what to do either."

"But you're so good at it."

She rolls her eyes. "Yeah, when I tell you to make me coffee or go with me to the kids' school events and put up with my precious driving. But this is a life choice that involves someone else's heart. The way I see it, since you're being stubborn and not doing what you should, you have two options. Take some time to just be friends and tell her when you're comfortable, or ask her out, rip off the Band-Aid, and tell her on your first date and risk losing something before it starts. Either way, she will need to know."

I don't know exactly what answer I was expecting when I told her everything, but I didn't think she would give me two alternatives with the same result.

I cringe when I think about adding more to the story. "So, I already asked her out once. And she said no."

Kacey lowers her eyebrows and squints at me with the most scornful scowl on her face. "She said no, dude. Why are you even thinking about trying again?"

"Because I really like her!"

"But you forget that this inner torture you've got going on in that bald head of yours about whether you should try dating her or leave her alone is one *thousand* percent self-induced, and you refuse to change anything."

The corner of my mouth quirks up. "So, I could be living in Alderaan, but I'm stuck on Hoth. By choice."

"Yeah," she says as her eyes dart back and forth without a clue about what I'm saying. "Exactly."

No one likes Hoth. The only positive of staying on that ice planet is that it's preserving my dignity to some extent. Kacey will never understand that.

"Yep. Okay. Thanks, sis."

"Happy to serve. Although, I'm not sure if anything got through that shiny shell of a head." She hops off the barstool. "Okay, Mama's gonna finish her nap on the orgasmic bed. May the Force be with you."

I put the empty mugs in the sink and rinse them off. My stomach has yet to recover from the sinking battleship of disappointment. Besides the debacle with Anna, things are finally good in my life right now. I feel good.

Nichole makes me feel good.

She's supposed to clean my house again in a couple days once Kaden's well. I'll make her lunch when she's done, and I'm going to try again. Screw all the reasons I shouldn't do it. I'm so close.

A ham and Swiss sandwich with french fries: The lunch of champs.

Nichole told me she likes a sandwich with a side of fries. Thanks to my bachelor diet, I have a bag in the freezer that I pop in the air fryer.

Once she finishes cleaning, I invite her to sit at the island with me and I slide the plate toward her. She shimmies her shoulders and smiles with approval. *I win.*

"Is Kaden feeling better?" I ask as I eat from my own plate.

Nichole nods. "Yesh, thank odd," she says through a mouthful of sandwich. "*Oh.* Is been oh ong ince I las ay."

"When *did* you eat last?"

She looks up to the ceiling and thinks, then swallows her bite. "Last night."

"Last night? No wonder you're chowing down! I could never go that long without eating."

She quirks an eyebrow. "You callin' me Jabba the Hutt?"

I snort on a gulp of water, and now I'm worried I just insulted her. "What? No. I was just saying I understand why you'd be hungry."

She snickers and waves a hand at me. "I'm just messin' with you."

I chuckle. Another reason why I've let her into my heart.

The silence expands with each second as I take a bite of my own sandwich, and it's painful. I want to ask personal questions. Get to know her like Kacey suggested. Beat around the bush and see if there's any chance she's changed her mind. Or if Kaden's father is involved in his life.

"So, I have a question."

The corner of Nichole's mouth tilts up. "I have an answer." She pauses to rethink her words. "I hope."

Good God, she's adorable. "Can I ask what happened with Kaden's dad?"

She grunts in a way that tells me my question wasn't a big deal. She puts a hand over her mouth as she chews. "We were actly mual fends," she says through her food, and I have to hold back a laugh. She swallows before continuing. "I guess you could say he was my high school sweetheart. Married *way* too young." She adds with hand gestures, "I don't recommend getting married out of high school. Not a good idea."

"I'll keep that in mind."

"Anyway. Kaden was over a year old when Jared started working late out of nowhere." She raises her eyebrows and shakes her head at whatever memory she's about to divulge. "When it starts happening every day for two weeks, then you find a bra that's not yours in the back seat of his car, you know somethin' ain't right."

Sounds too familiar. When Anna was having her affair, she had the gall to do it under our own roof. "I found a—" She turns shy and reserved, seemingly almost embarrassed to admit it. "—condom wrapper on the floor next to the bed that made the sirens blare in my mind. I knew that was the biggest indicator, and it was devastating. The person who's supposed to be your life partner decides they don't want to be that anymore is a stomp to the innards. I got a brand-new mattress after she left.

"He couldn't hide it," she continues. "He promised he'd cut it off and it wouldn't happen again, blah blah blah. Then I look over at his phone when he gets a text one day, and the contact name is from 'Larry Work.' Which, I know you're thinking sounds legit, but when it's a photo of a woman in a scantily clad bikini and she asks what he wants to do to her, the math don't math." She scoffs. "It felt like if Rey decided Kylo Ren wasn't good enough so she chose Finn." I can't suppress my grin as she rethinks her analogy. "Except Kylo Ren dies, but you get the point."

I cringe. She tells the story like it's something to laugh about years down the road. I would join in the humor if I wasn't thinking about how to kill someone telepathically.

I've never been officially divorced. I never had a child with Anna that I had to raise alone. I can at least tell her parts of my story so she can understand that. It doesn't mean I have to tell her the whole truth right now.

"God, I'm sorry Nichole." I clear my throat. "I hate that I can say I know how that feels. I was cheated on too. She decided her dental patient was more appealing, so once I found out about that, I kicked her out. No suitcase or anything."

Nichole's eyebrows shoot straight to her hairline. "You kicked her out?" She lets out a deep, boisterous laugh. "Boy, you be ruthless!"

I flash a confident smirk. "I know."

"I commend you. What a hoe." She wipes her mouth with a napkin, and I'm laughing hard. My sister asked if she could beat up a hoe, and now Nichole just called my soon to be ex-wife one too. She had the boldness to tell it like it is, and I like her even more.

"The worst part of it was that it was during a time in my life when I needed support." I swallow hard. "My dad died five years ago, and I'm still recovering."

Nichole frowns. "Aw, Pete, I'm so sorry. You guys were close?"

I smile reflectively with the memories of being in the garage, working a saw, the smell of sawdust, paint all over our hands. "Yeah. We were." I point toward the garage. "We used to do a lot of projects together."

"Like working on cars or something?"

I shake my head. "Nah. Something more unique than that. Something you probably wouldn't find at home goods stores or art shows."

Nichole's mouth forms an O, full of intrigue. "Can I see it?"

Something about this feels like a big step. Even I can barely muster the courage to go into the garage and be invaded by all the familiar smells and old projects. She wants to step into that part of my life. Willingly.

"Yeah, of course."

She follows me to the door leading to the garage, and I don't hesitate when I open it for her. Her smile spreads into one of awe and amazement. She examines one diorama at a time on all four shelves lining two of the walls.

"Pete," she finally says breathlessly. "These are . . . incredible." She gasps and points at one. "*The Princess Bride!*" Then does it repeatedly. "Mickey Mouse on that one ship! *Felix the Cat* clock! Tweety and Sylvester! *Lady and the Tramp* with the spaghetti!" Her gasp goes deeper when she sees one with the Death Star in it. "That's my favorite, hands down!"

I fold my arms and simply watch how excited she gets with each one. It feels good that someone cares enough about my background to want to see everything Dad and I did together for years. Nichole is genuinely interested.

The only downside to that is, it's making me fall for her harder.

She points to the wooden box on the table that's been there for two years. "Is this something you're working on?"

I'm slightly disappointed that I still haven't figured out what to do with that. "No. That was my dad's next diorama before he died. I haven't touched it since."

Nichole's eyebrows furrow. "How come?"

I shrug. "It didn't feel right working on it without him. He must've had a plan, but I don't know what it was."

She steps closer to the table and studies the box. "You should do something with it. Like, something in his honor."

"Like what?"

She shrugs. "Anything. You'll never know what he wanted to do with it, but you can finish it for him. Do something that you know would have meant something to him."

I ruminate on the idea. As silly as it sounds, I was afraid he would've been mad if I messed with his work in progress, as if he's still around somehow. Nichole has provided me with a different perspective. He's not around to do anything with it. The best person to create something profound is me.

Never in the last five years did I view it that way. She's completely changed that.

I need this woman in my life. I deserve her.

"Go out with me."

Nichole's head snaps in my direction. I caught us both off guard. I didn't mean to blurt it out, but I couldn't help it.

"What?"

I clear my throat. "Sorry. That came out of nowhere."

She huffs out her throaty laugh. "It really did."

"I'm serious, though." I step close enough to her that she's almost flush against my chest. "I know you had a horrible experience with your ex. I know you have a son to take care of. But I promise you'll never have to worry about me being unfaithful. And I promise I won't get in the way of you being a mom. I just hope you can trust that I will never break your heart. You're just . . ." I grip her shoulders. "You're just so freaking amazing."

Nichole looks like she's about to cry. Her walls are crumbling into dust, I know it. "You know, I kinda thought this was a date."

I rear back. "Really? How?"

"You fed me lunch and you're showing me your collection. It's like a scene in a rom-com."

"Did you *want* this to be a date?" I ask in a hushed voice.

She bobs her head in thought, and relents. "I mean, I'd hope if we went on a first date, it wouldn't be at your house with a sandwich and fries, but I'll take what I can get."

A simple yes or no to my question was all I wanted, but this banter is a fun game too. "Okay. What is a dream date for Nichole Tyler?"

She hums for a moment, blushing and trying very hard to hide her excited smile. "It would involve coffee, a walk by the water at sunset. And just talking."

Wow. A woman that doesn't expect a lavish, expensive first date. That's a first.

"So, if I planned out that dream date, just the way you want it, would you consider going out with me?"

She averts her gaze to the concrete floor. The pause has me sincerely worried she'll say no. But that feeling obliterates when she smiles coyly. "Maybe."

My cheeks heat. My heart pounds. My vocal cords want to cheer and shout.

I asked her out again.

She said yes this time. At least, that's how I'm taking it.

Apparently, all I had to was show off a little. Just call me Han Solo.

"Okay." I chuckle. "Great. That's great. Yeah. I'll text you."

She rolls her bottom lip between her teeth, containing her beaming smile. "Great."

The silence and romantic tension expand between us as we stand in front of each other. Two people blushing and just plain excited to go on a date. I want to reiterate that she won't regret this, that this can go as fast or slow as she wants, that I will build the freaking Millenium Falcon for her if she wanted me to.

That might be a bit much right now.

She finally breaks the quiet. "I should get going."

"Oh. Right." I clear my throat. "I'll help you with that."

Once we get her stuff packed and loaded into the trunk of her car, it's awkward again, just like when I brought groceries to her house. Now that we're going on a date, I don't know what to do with myself. A hug might be too forward, a handshake is too formal, and a kiss on the cheek is too familiar.

Nichole has gotten me more twisted up than any other woman in my life.

She decides to give me a one-armed hug. A proper choice. "I'll see you later."

I return the hug, and it feels so freaking good, just like the full hug I gave her weeks ago. I don't remember the last time I held a woman I had genuine feelings for. This time, it's harder to let go.

A bright red Mustang turns onto my street from the top of the hill. I immediately recognize it. My insides go rigid.

I have to get Nichole out of here. I practically shove her into her car. She puts on a weirded-out expression with this sudden change in behavior. Which is fine, because I'm not going to explain it to her.

Thankfully, she backs out of the driveway before the Mustang shows up, engine purring. Anna slides out of her car, prim and proper. Her bright blonde hair is neatly combed back in a ponytail and her compression shirt and workout leggings show off every inch and curve of her bone-thin body.

"Who was that that just drove off?" she asks snidely as she walks up my driveway like it's still hers.

"I don't believe that's any of your concern."

Anna hums, turning to Nichole's car that's just reached the end of the street. "Really? Kinda looked like a girlfriend." She turns back to me with a devilish grin. "Does she know you're still married?"

The realization stings, but I push it aside. "Do *you* know that I don't care what you think?"

She pushes past me through the front door. "I won't take long. I just came to pick up some more clothes, since you left me in the street with nothing but the clothes on my back."

I shut the door with fury brewing within me. "Fine, but you're leaving as soon as you're done."

She grunts and mumbles something that I'm sure is insulting, then stomps her way upstairs. I would call the cops and have her escorted off my property, but, as she had to remind me, we're still married. She's still entitled to the house and her belongings.

Having her here, I make a decision. I refuse to burden Nichole with this situation. I don't want her to have any part of this. I need to protect her from the drama, and from Anna.

This will have nothing to do with our relationship or how I feel about her.

This is my problem, and my problem only.

Chapter 11

Nichole

I called an emergency Felicia meeting at Caffeinated Vino after I left Pete's house. My first instinct was to text them in all caps that they were right and I have a date, but I want to see their reactions firsthand.

Because I can't contain myself, I'm the first one there in our usual booth. The lights have dimmed and the bar has opened, so I don't hesitate to order a lemon drop.

Becca and Taryn rush in and practically run to the booth. "We never have emergency Felicia meetings!" Becca exclaims. "What's going on?"

"I think I know what it is," Taryn suggests, clasping her ringed fingers in front of her on the table. "But we should guess, just to spice things up."

"There can't be a lot of options," Becca remarks. "She's smiling, so it's good news."

"Wow, Felicia, I totally hadn't guessed that on my own," Taryn lays on the sarcasm thick.

Becca smacks her on the arm, then turns back to me, humming thoughtfully. "Either you earned enough money for Kaden's plane ticket . . ."

"That I did," I confirm. "But that's not the reason for this meeting."

"You're making way more money now. . ."

I shake my head.

"Or something happened with Pete."

I nod vigorously.

Taryn slaps the table in quick succession, eyes bulging from her head. "What? Speak, Felicia!"

My smile reaches my ears and I squeeze my shoulders together. "I think Pete just asked me out."

Becca's waiting to be excited and Taryn doesn't seem convinced yet. I was trying to be subtle and not come across as a braggart, especially with the way Becca feels about this situation.

"You *think*?" Taryn asks with heavy doubt. "He either did or he didn't."

"Guys can do it in a roundabout way that can make us feel stupid, *Felicia*," Becca emphasizes to Taryn, then turns to me. "I thought you were convinced you weren't gonna go out with him."

"Yeah, you shot him down last time," Taryn notes. "So what changed?"

He wormed his way into my heart, that's what changed. Recalling the series of events has me on cloud nine all over again. "He showed me some projects he and his dad worked on when he was alive, we were chatting about them, and he just blurted 'go out with me.'"

Becca dramatically clutches her chest. "That's so sexy. It's literally my dream for someone to say that to me."

"Then he asked what my dream date was. Then he talked about how he knows I've been hurt in the past, and that he would never do that to me. And told me I'm amazing."

Becca throws her head back. "You *are* amazing. But if you said no again, I will legit smack you upside the head." She smiles mischievously, clearly joking. "Then I'll take my shot at him."

"Careful," I say in a playful warning tone. "Those are fighting words."

"Okay, you must have said yes this time because we know our Felicia ain't stupid and wouldn't pass up a good man," Taryn interjects.

"I know, I was just being subtle." I throw myself into a fit of giggles. "Pete Daley asked me out."

I'm still dumbstruck. I'm a mom, my ex is still involved, I've had some horrible dating experiences, and I've been single for eight years. Through all of that, he still wants to go out with me. He wouldn't have tried so hard to convince me if he had a problem with any of my baggage.

I like him. A lot.

More importantly, I trust him.

I shoot my arms in the air. "I HAVE A DATE WITH PETE DALEY!"

Becca and Taryn cheer like we're at a Kane Brown concert. None of us care the slightest that we're destroying the calm, quiet atmosphere. There's no girls' night if we can't celebrate properly.

Becca puts down her glass after taking a sip. "Hey, so, can you let me know if he has a single brother?"

Taryn smacks her arm. "No, I call dibs!"

"While you guys flip a coin to decide who gets the next single hunk, I'm gonna be on a date with *Pete Daley*!" I shout with my glass raised.

We clink glasses again. Then I remember something. Pete asked me out, but I never actually confirmed anything.

God, I'm an idiot.

"Wait!" I hold up my hands. "I messed up."

Taryn and Becca wait for me to continue, confused by my sudden light bulb moment.

I say each word slowly and sprinkle in some shame in my tone. "I don't think I gave him an answer."

Taryn's brow raises. "Whaddya mean you didn't give him an answer?"

"I was being all flirty and said 'maybe.' Not yes."

Becca leans forward and lightly bumps her forehead on the table repeatedly. "Felicia!" She groans, then raises her head while laughing. "You called an emergency Felicia meeting only to find out you didn't actually say yes?"

"Do it right now," Taryn demands, pointing at my phone on the table.

"What do I even say?"

"Just tell him that you just realized saying 'maybe' wasn't a solid answer and that you would be over the moon to go out with him." She slaps the table. "Boom, problem solved."

"Can't I just wait for him to text me so I don't look too eager?"

"For crying out loud, stop worrying so much!" Becca snaps. "Making sure you didn't confuse him isn't being eager."

"Well, he seemed to take it as a yes, so maybe it's fine."

"Oh good Lord, gimme your phone." Becca snatches it from my hand. "I'll text him for you."

I launch across the table to retrieve my phone from her. "No, no, I'm a grown woman. I can handle this."

"Sure," Taryn drawls out.

"He's gonna think I'm an idiot and change his mind," I grumble as I pull up my messages.

"Have another drink," Taryn suggests. "You're not gonna care after another lemon drop."

She orders me a second drink, and each sip proves her right. It makes sense why alcohol is called "liquid courage."

I'm fighting happy giggles as I send the text.

Me: I don't know if my answer was good enough, so lemme try again. Yes, Pete, I'd love to go out with you.

He replies within a few seconds.

Pete: I thought we established that, but thank you for clarifying ;)

I didn't expect him to respond so soon. I figured since he sacrificed so much of his afternoon to feed me, talk with me, and show me his dad's projects, he'd be too busy catching up on work to even bother looking at his phone. Cece expects him to do a lot of the heavy lifting, and he might have other clients to deal with on top of it all. Reminds me of Linda and her unrealistic expectations with my cleaning.

"See?" Becca answers after I read them his response. "He still wants to go out with you. Have some faith next time, woman."

Becca and Taryn chat among themselves while I go back to texting my date.

Me: Anytime, Captain.

Pete: How does Friday night sound?

Me: That sounds great. Where do you wanna go?

Man, maybe I need to drink more often. Normally, I wait to confirm that someone can watch Kaden before I make plans, but I'm so mellow and ballsy that I've decided I'll figure that out later. He always has Camilla and Oscar, or Becca and Taryn can hang out at my place. Kaden's fine. All is well. I have a date that actually has promise.

Pete: It's a surprise. You like surprises, right?

Me: They're my favorite.

Pete: Good. Wear something you would wear on a date, but dress comfortably.

Me: Unfortunately I incinerated all the clothes I wore on previous dates.

Pete: That bad, huh?

Me: I was trying to burn the memories with them.

Pete: Understood. Then pick something you look good in while being comfortable?

Me: Not sure if that narrows it down . . .

Pete: Well I guess you'll find out ;)

Me: does any of it involve me knocking stuff over?

Pete: it's not totally out of the question. See you Friday. I promise you'll love it.

It's a promising date, and that takes all the self-control I have to not jump and wrap my legs around him. Of course I'm going to love it.

"So he says to wear something that's comfortable and makes me look good," I say to my girls.

Becca rubs her hands together. "Does this mean we're coming over to help pick out an outfit?"

"Felicia, we do that every single time she has a date," Taryn notes, "of course we're coming over for this one!"

We clink glasses one last time and continue to celebrate with more drinks.

This is all a dream. It has to be. He's the man of my dreams, and he's choosing me.

"Sooooo," Becca draws out, "I'm guessing the goal tonight is to show off your voluptuous butt?"

Friday night has arrived and I haven't even picked an outfit. I had to have my Felicias help me, and not just because I asked them to watch Kaden and Oscar since Camilla had to take care of her mother. They only agreed because they wanted payment for watching two boys instead of just one. Then Knox decided to join in on the chaos because he wanted to hang out with Taryn while Katie had other plans. Three babysitters and two boys is going to be a riot.

This date, above all others, is making me sweat the most. I may have liked the other guys, but none of them made me this anxious. Pete has no clue how nervous he makes me. Like, *really* nervous.

"Well yeah," I answer, smacking my booty in my good-butt jeans. "Pete's gotta see how good it is."

"At least pair it with something that has *Star Wars* on it," Taryn suggests, moving about my clothing-filled bedroom to my overstuffed closet with a glass of whiskey in her hand. "Y'all can geek out together."

Becca takes multiple items from the closet and lays an ultimate *Mandalorian* representation on the bed: a Grogu beanie with the Yoda ears, a clutch with Grogu on it, and a sweater dress with Grogu drinking a mug of coffee, and a pair of matching leggings. "If you're gonna geek out, I say go all out. And it still shows off your booty."

As if I needed a valid excuse to flaunt it.

"Whelp, at least it'll be a memorable date."

Multiple knocks sound on the bedroom door as I'm bent over trying to pull the sweater dress over my head. Becca laughs at my grunting and Taryn watches while pressing a cheek on her palm.

"Guys, the ladies are busy," Knox calls from the other side of the door with no authority in his voice whatsoever. "Get back here."

"Knoxy Loxy, your babysitting skills need some heavy improvement!" Taryn snaps.

He isn't able to do much else, though, because Kaden bursts in, Oscar trailing behind him.

Taryn and Becca scream and practically trip over my clothes to close the door. I'm still bent over with my dress half on and my turquoise bra on full display, and I'm equally horrified.

"Why didn't you lock your door?" Becca asks.

"What are you guys doing?!" I yell through the muffled barrier of the top. I quickly right myself and pull the dress all the way down off my head.

"We thought of an idea for my science fair project!" Kaden shouts excitedly. He and Oscar then chug from their cans of energy drinks. I'll have to scold my Felicias for giving them those so late in the day; they'll never sleep.

"Unless you're here to fill me up with more whiskey, we politely ask you to vacate the premises for a couple minutes," Taryn says in a calm, authoritative tone.

Kaden and Oscar exchange a confused glance. "What's 'premises'?"

"Leave the bedroom!" Becca enunciates as she shoves them out the door and closes it. She's yet to stop laughing.

"What is it with boys and not having boundaries?" I groan in frustration.

"Can we come back in now?" Oscar calls from the other side of the door.

"Yes, children, you can," I grumble.

The boys burst in as they did before, laughing with the silliness they feed off from each other.

"Next time, can ya wait for permission after knocking before bursting into my room?" I snap with my hands on my hips. I know this moment is one I will be able to look back on and laugh about, but the time is not now, because I'm pretty sure I've sweated out my entire body's weight in water, and my tightly curled hair is sticking straight up from my head.

"Yes, Miss Tyler," Oscar answers, the ever so politely raised child.

"Now what's up?"

"I believe he said he has an idea for the science fair project," Becca assists with a playful portion of cockiness.

"And it doesn't involve whiskey," Kaden deadpans to Taryn.

"Then why bother with science at all?" she replies with a shrug, and hops on the edge of the bed.

"I'm kinda doing something like that, though," he says.

"What is it?" Becca leans in to listen intently.

Kaden twists behind him to whisper, "Drumroll, Oscar." Oscar rolls his tongue and imitates banging drumsticks on a drum. "I want to test whether coffee or energy drinks increase productivity."

Coffee and energy drinks? Is it sad I'm actually excited about this topic simply because it involves caffeine?

I clap with enthusiasm. "That sounds great, baby!"

Taryn points a finger at Kaden. "Now for *that* I will happily be a test subject."

Becca shoots her hand straight up. "Oh! Oh! Me too! I don't do energy drinks, but coffee is my jam!"

"Okay, I gotta do my makeup." I pat Kaden's cheeks. "But that sounds great. Just tell me what you need, okay?"

"The experiment starts now!" Oscar announces. The boys raise their cans with a war cry and take off down the hallway.

"Did you guys really have to give them energy drinks?" I whisper shout. "It's almost six o'clock at night!"

Becca raises her hands in surrender. "Blame Knox. He brought some and gave them to Kaden and Oscar, and by the time we noticed, they were the annoying monkeys from the *Super Mario World* games."

Not that I know what she's talking about, but two ten-year-olds acting like monkeys is never a good sign.

"Knox should never have children," Taryn mumbles as she heads for the bedroom door.

"Do your makeup, we'll take away their drinks," Becca commands while following Taryn into the hallway.

Yeah. Right. Makeup. Need to look presentable for my hot date. Need to stop sweating so my makeup will stick to my face.

Need to show off the goods.

Chapter 12

Pete

Calm down, Petey. She's nothing like Anna. Breathe and enjoy it. When all else fails, light a cigar and pour yourself some whiskey.

That's what I imagine Dad would say if he were still alive. He could make the worst situation into a funny one. "Laughing is better than crying," he'd say. That always helped Mom, too, whenever she was in a panic.

Thanks to her, I may have inherited some of that, because various potential date-ruining scenarios keep springing up in my mind.

What if my car breaks down?

What if I want to kiss her and we knock teeth instead?

What if we have nothing to talk about?

What if I get an upset stomach and blow up the bathroom?

Yeah. It's clear I haven't been on a date in a while. My beard is damp from sweat and I know my head is shining with it too.

I got an earful from Kacey when I told her I was going on a date. "Your funeral," she said, "but I'm also excited that you're happy. I'll bring the kids and we can pick an outfit for you."

I didn't really know how to respond to the variety of emotions she wasn't able to narrow down, but I can't reject help when I need it.

Charlotte digs through my walk-in closet like Yoda searching through Luke's storage container on Dagobah, throwing things aimlessly. She grabs a loose, black robe from a hanger. "What about this?"

"That's my Darth Vader costume."

She wrinkles her nose. "You need new clothes. And a life."

Couldn't agree more, young Padawan.

Lucas runs into the bedroom from the master bathroom and I'm hit with a heavy scent like a brick wall. I'm just glad it's not BO.

"Luke, are you wearing my cologne?" I ask through a fit of coughs.

He puts on his puppy dog eyes and whines, "No."

"Really? It smells awfully familiar."

"*You* smell awfully familiar." He makes a silly face.

"Lucas, stay out of your uncle's stuff." One sniff and Kacey rears back. "Holy crap, did you bathe in the whole bottle?"

"No."

"You smell like a cab driver," Charlotte says.

"You saying I smell like a cab driver?" I mock being offended.

"You don't even know what they smell like," Lucas argues with his sister.

Kacey turns from taking out a suit jacket from the closet and pushes her kids into the hallway. "Okay, have your enlightening conversation outside. Don't touch any of his stuff, or I'll haunt your dreams."

The pounding of running feet recedes down the hallway and down the stairs. Kacey turns back to me and examines my outfit in progress—black slacks and white dress shirt open at the collar.

She hands me the jacket. "I'm pretty sure you won't have to put on cologne. Lucas practically wafted it all over you."

"Well, I'm sweating a little bit. Wouldn't hurt to use some more."

She wrinkles her nose. "No. It's kinda suffocating. Let's not choke your date to death." She wipes the jacket free of dust and fuzz with a proud smile. "I'm happy to see you happy, though."

I *am* happy. Finally, genuinely happy. More than I have been in years. Things feel lighter. Freer. I never paid attention to how much Anna weighed me down. Her affair was the most emasculating thing she could've done.

My first date with Anna was at a movie theater. We barely talked; it felt like we didn't get much conversation in at all. I didn't know a whole lot at nineteen years old. Because I haven't dated since then, I want tonight to go smoothly. I'm not about to screw it up by involving Nichole in my problems.

"I'll tell her. Just not now."

"You really need to tell her sooner than later. If she's been through as much as you say, you don't want to hide anything."

I blow a frustrated breath. "I've told you why I don't want to tell her right now. The situation with Anna is *my* problem."

She sighs in disappointment. "I hope this is worth it."

I chuckle softly. "I think she is."

She leans in closer to my face. "Kiss her real good," she whispers seductively.

"Ugh. I'd accept that advice if it wasn't coming from my sister."

"It's like you don't know me. I have no filter." She pats my cheek before leaving my bedroom.

"Is it possible we might be too close?" I call after her.

I give myself a once-over in the mirror and take a deep breath. Roll my head side to side, then take another deep breath.

I got this.

On the way to Nichole's place, I pick up the bouquet of roses I ordered ahead of time. She's going to love them. A hopeless romantic I am.

When she answers the door, her girlfriends crowd right behind her. I barely notice them when I take in Nichole's full-blown Grogu-themed outfit, and makeup done so perfectly that she could be a magazine model. She's the perfect combination of beautiful and flat-out adorable. I adored her the moment I saw her, but seeing her outside of her cleaning gig, her raw, unprofessional self is a sight to behold.

I don't know if I should compliment her at this moment; I was hoping to not do it in front of an audience.

I hand her the small bouquet. "These are for you."

Nichole coos as she takes and sniffs them. "You're too sweet. Thank you."

Becca grabs the flowers and retreats to the kitchen. Taryn follows her.

"Is that your boyfriend?" Kaden calls from the living room.

If Nichole's blushing, it's not showing in the dimness of the outdoor light. "You want to come say hi?" she asks.

Great. An audience and a judge.

Pounding feet sound behind her, then Kaden squeezes under her arm to stand in front. "Hi."

"Hey, bud. How's it going?"

"Oscar and I are gonna pretend we're fighting Poison Fiends with the guns you got me," he announces.

My chest swells with pride. Approval from my date's child is now what counts as success in my book. "Cool. I hope you kill lots of them. Maybe I can help you with my own gun sometime."

"You have a *Fortnite* gun?" He tilts his head curiously. "I thought you liked *Star Wars*."

"I do. But I got an E-11 Blaster Rifle too."

He gasps. "That's so cool! Can I see it?"

Jackpot.

"Sure, I'll bring it by sometime." I turn to Nichole and wink. I absolutely plan on coming back. With the way she grins and observes this interaction, she's agreeing.

"Yes!" Kaden turns to Nichole and whispers something that makes me even prouder. "I like him."

She pats his back as he runs inside toward another kid that I'm guessing is Oscar. I just successfully earned the approval of a child I barely know. I'm officially awesome.

"You have a *Fortnite* gun?" Nichole asks in a low voice.

"Nope. But now I have to get one."

She giggles as she steps outside. I guide her to my car, my hand just hovering over her lower back. I can't say I mind the view. Greek goddesses ain't got nothing on Nichole.

"Have fun you two," Taryn calls with a lilt from the door.

"If you have any single friends, send them our way!" Becca adds.

Nichole and I have a good laugh. I take another second to look her over and be proud to call her my date. "You look beautiful."

She scoffs and waves a hand. "Nothing fancy, just a big sweater and leggings."

"You look beautiful in everything."

She tamps down her sheepish smile as I open the door for her. I breathe out the millionth nervous breath I've taken when I close her door. The way her makeup makes her eyes pop, her perfect dark brown skin, her smile that's so full of life, is more overwhelming than I expected. Now I'm just excited to start the car, because I have an added surprise for her.

I turn on the engine, and everything lights up, just like her eyes do when we talk *Star Wars*.

I basically converted the inside of my car to look like a spaceship. All of my floor mats were replaced with blue reflective ones. The darkness outside combined with the interior lights on the floor create the perfect ambience.

"Whoa!" Nichole's eyes scan the whole car, like a little kid in an amusement park. "This is so cool!"

I wink. "Prepare for takeoff, Miss Tyler."

Chapter 13

Pete

"What do you think of this one?"

Nichole said her dream date involved coffee, and I took it to a whole new level.

A bougie, popular coffee roastery in Seattle seemed perfect as a first stop. Nichole gets to drink coffee—mixed with alcohol—and doesn't have to pay for it. She deserves a nice night out.

She takes a sip from an espresso martini flight with a dried orange slice floating on top. I watch her fingers wrapped around the mini glass—dainty, slender, yet so hardworking that it's a wonder they're not covered in calluses. "I think . . . I've had so much caffeine my heart's gonna blow from my chest." She giggles a little drunkenly. Or nervously. I can't tell which is which. They sound the same. "Wanna catch it for me once it does?"

"As long as you catch mine too."

She clinks her glass with the one I just picked up with a dusting of cocoa powder. "Deal."

I take a sip of the concoction. It's bitter, as black coffee usually is. The espresso crema on top adds a smoothness. The cocoa adds flavor. Can't say I hate it.

"So," I start, licking the foam off my lips that I catch Nichole watching with a hardcore focus. I try not to chuckle so she isn't embarrassed that I notice her gawking. "Do you always have your friends watch Kaden?"

She smacks her lips after finishing her glass. "No. Oscar's mom lives next door and she watches the boys sometimes too. She needed someone to watch Oscar tonight so Becca and Taryn are watching both of them. Then, Taryn's friend Knox wanted to hang out with her and decided that he'd babysit with them."

Poor Becca, Taryn, and Knox. "Oh, I bet they'll have a blast."

"With the amount of energy drinks they've had, they're probably having a ball."

"Oh no, that's a bad combo." I slide my finger along the edge of an empty glass, imagining how those boys would get along with Lucas.

"Oh!" Nichole claps excitedly. "Which reminds me. Kaden told me he decided to test productivity in people drinking energy drinks and coffee for his science fair project. Taryn and Becca said they'd be guinea pigs for him, so more exploding hearts are in the near future." She giggles again. "And he decided to tell me this while I was trying to get my clothes on for this date."

I laugh. I laugh *hard*, and it feels incredible. I thought I was incapable of having fun and simply laughing when Anna left. Nichole has brought it back to life.

Kaden and I seemed to hit it off a little more, although I'll have to buy myself a *Fortnite* gun. It doesn't hurt that it's a good way to see more of Nichole in a less professional setting by spending time with her son.

Plus, I love coffee. I make it like a pro. I'm the perfect test subject.

"I would be down to be a guinea pig. If he wants."

She waves off the idea. "You don't have to if you don't want to. I don't want you to feel like you have to kiss up to my son. I think you've already won him over."

I may be kissing up just a little bit, but I can tell he's a good kid. I see a future with his mother. I don't know what it is with me when I'm around him, but I don't need to try all that hard. It feels so natural, just being his buddy. Being an uncle isn't quite the same as being a new man in a kid's life, but Kaden makes it easy. He's chill, resilient, and accepting. Not a lot of kids are like that.

"No, it actually sounds like fun. Just tell me what he needs." I down another espresso martini. "If it helps, I've had three espresso martinis and I could probably swim across Lake Washington."

"I'd pay to see you do it!" She leans forward as she chokes out more laughter, and I follow suit. Her laugh is contagious. I swear I haven't laughed this much in years, and she seems like she's having a wonderful time too.

Kacey is crazy. There's no way I can ever tell her about Anna.

"Well then." I lean in close, keeping my voice low and sultry in a way she won't be able to resist. "It's a good thing our next destination involves a lake."

"Please don't actually swim in the water!" Nichole shrieks as we run across the park to the beach of Lake Washington. "If you lose your heart in the water, I won't be able to save you! It's cold as balls!"

She has a point. It's the end of October. It's pitch-black in the middle of the park, and I'm afraid of leading us into a tree, so I use the flashlight on my phone to guide the way. We reach an area where some streetlamps dimly light the walkway in orange, as well as the wooden bridge that curves over the creek that flows into the lake, then all the way through to the boat launch.

Once the orange glow becomes clearer and we can actually see our feet, we slow our pace to a steady stroll. A romantic walk on the beach, just as she wished. But something is missing. We're not just two friends on a walk. This is a date.

I reach for her hand—my skin tingling with the touch that sends electricity through me, weakening my knees again—and intertwine our fingers. She runs her thumb over my hand, warmth trailing its path. Nothing has ever felt so right until now. That smile—God, that gorgeous, warm, movie-star smile—makes everything around us shrink into nothing. She looks at me like I'm the best thing that's ever happened to her. She's smiled at me this way before, but it hits differently now. Because this is real. And she's the best thing that's happened to me too.

I have no idea what I was thinking marrying Anna. What I had with her was nothing like this. I wish Dad were alive, just so I could tell him how sorry I was for ignoring his warning. And I shouldn't ignore warnings from my family.

Like my sister's advice to tell Nichole the truth. Tonight. When everything is so perfect. I want to hang onto that as long as possible.

We reach a patch of sand, where the city lights shimmer on the surface of the lake. Not a single person in sight.

Then I turn my head to see Nichole taking off her boots.

"Uh, what are you doing?"

She doesn't answer me. She rolls her leggings up to her knees, eyes on the beach the whole time, a wild and mischievous smile crossing her features.

"Wheeeeeeeee!" She squeals as she makes a beeline across the sand—which I'm sure is colder than Antarctica—straight toward the water, arms in the air.

"I was kidding about swimming!" I call after her. She only had three mini espresso martinis, but I didn't think about whether or not she's a lightweight. Or she's hyped on caffeine.

"I just want to see how cold it is!" Her bare feet make contact with the water for a total of a half second before she shrieks and hops from one foot to the other, a ripple of a wave splashing up to her ankles. "It's freaking freezing!"

I casually stroll closer to her. "I don't know what you were expecting. It's October."

"You know," she rasps, stepping back on the sand, then continues rapidly, "I hear of people doing the polar plunge in the winter and I wonder how people do it and I think maybe

I'm just a weenie and it's not that cold." She vigorously shakes her head. "Nope. It's polar bears and penguins cold."

I step out of my shoes and socks, and the sand is definitely colder than I expected. I crouch and dip my fingers in the water. "It's not that bad."

I'm lying. It's really cold.

"Then you must be a polar bear," she remarks with a neck roll.

"No, you just need to get acclimated." I scoop a handful of water in my hands. "Like this."

I throw it at her legs. She jumps and shrieks again.

"How dare you!" She kicks water directly at my face, and it turns into a battle. Water splashes everywhere, kicking and throwing scoops of it on each other, chasing each other and yelping whenever we're hit with the cold puddles and droplets.

I grasp the sleeve of her sweater dress when she tries to run away from me, and she stops. Her smile stays plastered on her face as she looks into my eyes.

"I'm pretty sure you've splashed enough water on my face to wash the makeup off," she comments with residual giggles.

"You don't need it," I say softly. The first time I ever saw her, she wasn't wearing makeup and riding the struggle bus, and I still thought she was beautiful. I don't care if she wears makeup or not.

I can't help it. I take her face in my hands, stroking her cheeks with my thumbs. She grasps my hands, reveling in the touch. I lean in, waiting for her permission. With the hitch in her breath and the fact that she hasn't withdrawn, I know she wants this as much as I do. The palpable energy between us is undeniable. I close the space, and my lips meet hers. Wet from the lake water, but soft and warm. When she opens for me, I kiss her deeper. All feeling within me reawakens, my heart pounding in my rib cage sending euphoria all over with each beat. I remain frigid, though, focused on the kiss itself and whether or not my lips are moving.

Her hands grip my shoulders, tightening on my skin each second this kiss lasts. We've been standing barefoot in the icy-cold water, yet I don't even notice it anymore. She was freezing just moments ago, but she's not moving out of the water either.

I finally break the kiss, my lips lingering just enough that we're barely touching. Her eyes are glazed over, off in a dream.

"I've been wanting to do that for a while."

She nods, still a little dazed. "Me too."

I take her hand in mine and lead her to a grassy area of the park. I seat us between some trees, gazing at the calm waters in silence. "Any of your other dates kiss you like that?" I ask with fake cockiness.

Nichole playfully smacks my arm. "Do you think we'd be here if they did?" She scoffs. "Most of my dates didn't even get to that point. One time it did and he was awful at it."

I lean in toward her. "Are you saying I'm like a breath of fresh air, Nichole?"

She blows a raspberry. "I don't think so."

I turn her toward me and kiss her again, but not as gently as the first time. I go a little rougher, making my mark on her face with my beard, nibbling her bottom lip. She pulls away from me, dazed and speechless.

"How about now?"

She lets out her infamous giggle. "Okay, you win."

I kiss her on top of her head and stare back out at the lake. The calming sound of water lapping on the shore and the docks is just loud enough to break through the quiet. Street and city lights glimmer on the surface like liquid glass. We sit there for a while and embrace the ambience. Arms wrapped around each other, taking in the view, and feeling honestly, truly content.

Chapter 14

Nichole

"I don't think I've been here when it's this dark," I say in a soft voice.

"I don't think I've been here at all."

I lift up my head faster than the speed of light to flash him a look of shock. "You've been here for years and you've never been to this park? It's like the one good thing about Creekside!"

"Because all I needed was *Star Wars*!"

I scoff. "You're such a guy."

"At least I had a hobby!"

"*Star Wars* is not a whole hobby!"

This goes on for hours, talking about everything from our childhoods to our marriages. Eventually, we get so cold that we have to go back to his car to warm up, but with no pause in conversation. He tells me he got into *Star Wars* when his mom took him and his sister to see the first movie at the drive-in theater. He ended up falling asleep halfway through, so he got hooked the second time around. I told him I didn't know what *Star Wars* was when I found the "Princess Leia in the gold bikini" costume online and wore it to Comic Con, and I felt a sense of friendship and community when everyone wanted photos with Black Leia. He told me how he lost a bet to his sister and had to wear a wedding dress in the middle of Seattle as she took a photo. I told him when I made an erotic cake for Becca to make her laugh when she was feeling down.

"So," I begin, after a brief pause in conversation, "what's one goal you want to accomplish in life?"

"Oh man, we're going deep."

"Yes, we are."

He clears his throat and breaks eye contact, adjusting himself more comfortably in his seat. "I guess this is more of a wish than anything."

"That works."

He chuckles. "I want to start over again and listen to my dad before I got married." He eyes his lap. "Before he died."

"What happened to him?" I quickly hold up my hands. "If you don't mind me asking."

He gives me an appreciative smile. "Heart attack. Which was odd because he was healthy as far as we knew." He chuckles sadly. "He was the best. I wish Anna could've seen that."

"Sounds like she was too self-absorbed."

"She was. Every year, Mom and Kacey and I get together and have dinner to remember him." He shakes his head. "She thought my life was revolving around his too much."

"Then what attracted you to her in the beginning?"

He takes a deep breath and catches a quick glimpse of my expression, like he's afraid I'm going to judge him for his answer.

Please. Like I have room to judge anyone about anything.

"She seemed like a genuinely sweet and caring person," he explains. "My family warned me that something wasn't right with her. But I didn't see it. I was in love. When we got married, it was like a switch flipped off, and I had no idea who she was. She always seemed jealous when Dad and I would hang out in the garage and work on those dioramas. We were selling some of them online, so I thought she would've appreciated that. It's not like we spent so much time on those projects that I neglected her. But apparently she thought I did." He chuckles. "What's funny is I had a feeling she would eventually cheat on me, especially when I had been grieving Dad for so long. Then she did, and I didn't feel bad about making her leave."

"Good on you for sticking up for yourself," I say through an admiring smile. "That must've been hard, though, since it was your wife."

"In the moment, I was so angry, it was easier than I thought." He laughs sardonically.

That brings me back to when Jared and I split up. Pete had the courage to not even let her redeem herself. An example I should've followed from the beginning. Maybe it wouldn't have been so gut-wrenching.

"When I found out my husband cheated, he seemed genuinely apologetic." I huff out a bitter laugh. "So I gave him a chance to make things right. Then he did it again. I was furious." I recall how he delivered the news, and he was so nonchalant about it. We had a baby together, and that was the time he decided he didn't want to be married. It was ridiculous.

"I decided that if he was going to cheat not just once, but twice, I'd never be able to trust him again. And in turn, I stopped trusting men altogether." I flap my hands. "When I started dating again, after all the horrible men I met, I felt like maybe I should have stuck to not trusting men and just being Kaden's mom. That's why I told you no the first time."

He nods, eyes closed as if listening intently. "I mean, I understood that you had bad experiences. I get how that can turn you off to wanting to be with anyone else." The corner of his mouth lifts. "But I'm glad you said yes. I hope I didn't make you feel pressured in any way."

What a sweet man, being so considerate and understanding of my feelings. No one has treated me with such respect; not even Jared.

I shake my head. "Not at all. I could only resist you for so long." I bring my hand to his bearded face. "You're a game changer, Pete."

He shuts his eyes tightly. "So are you," he says through a tight throat. Something in his expression changes. I can't put a finger on what it is. My first instinct is some sort of pain, but he's plowing right through it.

"But after all you've gone through . . . How do you know I'm not another Anna?"

Pete hums, thinking of a response. "When we were together, something always tugged at my gut. Like, something was off. I ignored it because I couldn't find a reason to doubt her. And we know how that turned out." His eyes meet mine, sincere and reassuring. "I didn't doubt it for a second with you."

That may be the hottest thing he's ever said to me.

Before I can think of anything else, I crash my lips with his in a searing kiss, letting him know how I feel about his statement.

I will never give him a reason to doubt me.

"Oh no! He's chasing us!"

"It's okay, I got 'em."

Pete shoots at Oscar, the acting Husk Monster, with the gun he promised he would get just for the alien fight taking over my small apartment. Oscar has managed to evade the Styrofoam bullets for the last hour.

Both Pete and Kaden needed to convince me to play along. I died within the first three minutes, and now I'm observing the battle before me in silence. It seems so effortless for Pete, like he's done this scenario a million times. If he's faking, he's doing a really good job of it. For once, though, I'm confident that he's not.

I can't stop thinking about our first date from last weekend. He remembered what my dream date was and included all the facets. It had been a long time since I felt so liberated and comfortable. Taking off my boots and going barefoot in the water is something I never imagined myself doing.

But he joined me. And he kissed me. A panty-melting one. The most romantic moment of my life.

When he came over today, he kissed me again. I didn't want him to stop. I don't know what he does to make his beard so soft, but that combined with his perfect, lush lips is addicting. I'm trying to think of ways I can keep his lips with me at all times.

A loud commotion brings me out of my reverie. Oscar falls to his knees, then falls face-first to the floor. Oh. They must have finally killed him.

Pete and Kaden cheer and high-five, lowering their guns and talking about how epic the battle was. They talk over each other excitedly while Oscar stays "dead" on the floor, like they don't even notice.

"Don't ignore the dead alien for too long," I point out, like having a fake alien in my house is an everyday occurrence. "His mom wants him back alive."

Pete leans down to help him up, practically using only one arm to lift his body back to life. His biceps flex with the motion, and it's *so hot*. How has it only been a week and I can barely contain myself?

"Well, Oscar, my apologies for killing you, but it's your fault you decided to be a Husk Monster."

Oscar shrugs. "It's fun! I'm the best at dodging bullets."

"You lasted a long time, man." Pete gives him a high five, and turns to Kaden to do the same. These kids already love him. Finally, I won the lottery.

He puts on his shoes and says his goodbyes to the boys, then I go with him to walk to his car. I barely spent any time with him today, but I was fine with it. He hit it off with my son, and that means more to me than anything.

Pete rests his hands on my waist. "You've got a pretty cool kid, hun." He lifts my chin with his forefinger. "And you are an incredible mom."

I blush from the compliment. I sometimes doubt my ability to be a good mom, even more so because I do it by myself. I've been a single mom since Kaden was two, but I still feel guilty occasionally. Sometimes I wonder if I should have stuck it out with Jared just so he could have a father in his life. A man for him to learn from. But what would it have taught my son if I stayed with someone I couldn't trust? What would it teach him about having self-respect? What kind of homelife is that for a child when you want to give them everything, and you want them to see what a happy couple looks like?

I couldn't raise him that way. I wasn't going to lie to him.

"Thank you," I reply bashfully. "Sometimes I wonder if I'm doing it right."

Pete leans against his car and folds his arms, examining me thoughtfully. "No parent is perfect, hun. You should see my sister with her kids. My niece sticks her finger in the dog's butt and my nephew treats cologne like it's soap."

I snort a laugh and hunch over. "Sounds like she has a lot of fun with those kids."

"You haven't heard nothin' yet." He hums in thought, as if something just occurred to him. "Actually—" His hands reach my shoulders, his thumbs skimming over the sleeves of my *Friends* T-shirt. "—what about you, my sister, my mom, and me go see a movie? They're running a *Star Wars* marathon at a theater in Seattle." He winks. "We can dress up."

Anxiety and panic flood my entire body. Meeting his family is a huge step for a couple who have only been dating for a week. Before Pete and I became an official couple, I'd known him for over a month. Seems like longer, but a month is not that long to know someone before meeting their family.

Their opinions might be the determining factor of this relationship.

Oh boy. This is a little crazy.

Wait a second. He met Kaden before we were a couple. That can also be a big deal when a single parent is back in the dating pool. Maybe just his sister and mother won't be so bad.

Okay. Panic subsiding. Maybe I can do this.

I bounce my eyebrows. "Dress up, huh? Are we doing a couples costume?"

He leans in, a sexy smile playing on his lips. "Yep."

He kisses me, slow and deliberate. How can I say no when I swear his lips are crafted with clouds and cotton?

"Okay, you convinced me," I say against his mouth.

He kisses me for a few more minutes before he leaves, and I'm wondering how this is all going to play out.

The theater happens to be inside another building. So when Pete and I take the escalator, and we're the only ones dressed to the nines in geekiness, I feel slightly out of place. But I remember I'm being geeky with my geeky boyfriend, so who cares?

I pulled out a wig to go as Princess Leia in my white Jedi clothes. Pete decided to dress as Obi-Wan Kenobi, and he did a great job with his brown robes and the belt holding his lightsaber.

Oh, and he's wearing a wig—the Ewan McGregor version. I'm tripping seeing him with hair after memorizing him as a bald man.

"You really go all out with your cosplay," I say.

Pete shrugs. "Go big or go home."

He intertwines his fingers with mine, sweaty from being nervous. I'm about to meet what's basically left of his family. They're going to decide what they think of me after tonight and I might just vomit.

"It's gonna be fun," he says, reading the thoughts showing on my face.

It's his family. Of course he thinks this will be fun.

Once we reach concessions, two women appear to be waiting for someone. One has charcoal-gray hair tied up in a bun, wearing a T-shirt with "Lucas" and "Charlotte" on it in the *Star Wars* font; the other is a skinny blonde with hair just touching her shoulders, wearing a T-shirt with the Death Star and the caption "That's no moon." If that's Pete's mom and sister, he looks like neither of them.

They turn, smile, and wave at him. I muster a smile through my nervousness.

"How did I know you'd be dressing up for this?" the blonde asks.

Pete feigns being offended. “It’s like you don’t know me!”

The older woman turns to me and motions to her kids. “You see what I’ve lived with for thirty plus years?” She laughs and goes for a hug. “I’m Sherri.”

Hugging me the first time we meet? That’s . . . super kind. “I’m Nichole.”

“Nice to meet you, Nichole!”

The blonde leans in for a hug too. “And I’m Kacey. I’m not exactly proud to call Pete my brother, but I don’t have much of a choice.” She turns to him and cackles.

Pete waves her off. “Don’t listen to her. She doesn’t like admitting to love.”

Kacey holds up her hands. “I’m just glad I have a kid-free night! Lucas and Lottie give me a run for my money.”

That explains the names on Sherri’s shirt.

Sherri motions between me and Pete. “I love that you both dressed up for this. That’s adorable!”

“Yeah,” Kacey says suspiciously. She gives Pete the stink eye. “Just what you were looking for, right, Pete?”

Her tone and the hidden message throw me off. Sherri doesn’t seem bothered by it, so I must be going crazy. I’m just hypersensitive to their views toward me, and I’m preparing for all negative comments and looks. Yeah, that’s all it is.

Pete chuckles sardonically, pulling me tightly to his side. “Well yeah! It’s not like a lot of women are *Star Wars* people.”

“I’m not a *Star Wars* person at all,” Kacey tells me, “but I really wanted to meet you. Pete has literally been gushing about you.” She scoffs and rolls her eyes playfully. “It’s disgusting.”

He smiles bashfully, admitting guilt with that simple look. "Has he now?" I ask.

He shrugs. "Maybe a little bit."

"And I only know because I eavesdrop on their phone conversations," Sherri admits like it's nothing.

Kacey groans. "I always forget about that."

"I'm gonna get some popcorn," Sherri says, moving to the concessions line. "Anyone want anything?"

"A medium popcorn and a water," Kacey answers. "If I don't have water, then the salt will make me look like a beluga." She grabs Pete's hand and practically drags him with her, like a kid in trouble. "We'll see you at the seats."

She doesn't have an issue with me. It's him. What did he do?

"So how are things going with Pete?" Sherri asks. "He told me that you have a son. Do they get along?"

Part of me worries that she's asking this to determine whether Pete would be fit to be a stepfather, therefore judging the fate of our relationship.

I need to knock that off. I just need to go with the flow and let them get to know me. She and Kacey care for Pete; I have to appreciate that to some extent.

"Things are great," I answer enthusiastically. "He and Kaden are basically best friends. They were playing with toy guns the other day in my apartment and they had a blast."

Sherri puts on an adoring look. "That's great!"

"Oh, and he showed me those 3D dioramas in his garage. They're incredible!"

Sherri goes rigid. My entire body breaks out in a sweat. If I offended her, I'm a dead woman.

"Oh," she finally says, still in a state of shock. "He showed you the dioramas? All the ones he did with his dad?"

I swallow hard. I decide to speak from the heart, because it's all true. I want her to know I'm sincere. "Yeah. He showed me the one his dad was working on before he died, and I was giving him some ideas on how he can finish it." I shake my head and reach out to touch her arm. "Your husband was an incredible artist. So is Pete."

Sherri seems to be suppressing a smile, her eyes darting about as if she doesn't know what to say, or how to accept the compliment about her late husband. While she takes a million years to respond, I'm doing everything I can to hide the fact that I'm panicking. The sweat has now cascaded from my back to my butt. I should've brought powder.

Finally, her smile breaks through, bright and warm. "Wow. You must be truly special to him."

I keep my smile plastered to my face. "What?"

"Pete's never shown those to anyone," she remarks. "And he's been stuck on that project for five years. Refused to do something with it." The way she grasps my arm so affectionately calms me down immediately. "I'm glad he found you. You are exactly what he needs."

She moves ahead of me in line, keeping a knowing smile on her face. I stay frozen in place, completely stunned and repeating the nicest thing anyone's said to me in my mind.

Chapter 15

Nichole

Pete invited me and my girls over for dinner, including his mom and sister. And Kevin, his single business partner, because he wanted to help Taryn and Becca see that there *are* good men out there. "I'll throw them a bone," he had said.

Becca and Taryn can't stop spinning in circles in total awe at the bright front room with the Stormtrooper outfits; impeccably clean and modern furniture (thanks to yours truly); a clean, dark-painted dining room table in the middle of the dining room; and a small bar full of dust-free glasses and alcohol (also thanks to yours truly). Kaden doesn't even notice it when he races toward the kitchen where Kacey's kids must be, then they're off playing before we know it. In the last month since Pete and I have been dating, Kaden and her kids have gotten along super well.

"You get to clean this place?" Taryn asks in shock.

"He be bougie," Becca adds, impressed. "Imagine living here, Felicia."

I wince. "As wonderful as that sounds, I'm not excited about always cleaning this place. It's a huge house."

"Then make him help you," Taryn suggests in a low voice. "It's called partnership."

Speaking of partnership, Pete walks in from the back lawn, the delicious scent of hot charcoal wafting inside, with a man equally as handsome, who I'm guessing is Kevin. Brown hair combed over to one side, slight five o'clock shadow, a white T-shirt and shorts. His shirt lifts up to give us a sneak peek of his abs as he takes a sip from his beer bottle.

Becca just gives him a welcoming smile and a shy wave. Taryn, on the other hand, does everything she can to not make any sort of eye contact with the man.

"Hey, ladies," Pete greets us. He gives me a kiss. "This is Kevin, my business partner."

Taryn is shy, as usual, but once she lifts her eyes and sees Kevin's handsome face, they don't move. At all. Becca shakes his hand, a light of hope shining in her eyes. Unfortunately, with the way Kevin's eyes are roving over Taryn head to toe, Becca might be out of luck. Kevin is polite to all of us, but he's laser focused on Taryn.

"So how long have you known Pete?" Kevin asks us, even though he's definitely asking Taryn directly.

We chat as we walk into the kitchen, where Kacey and Sherri are making potatoes, roasted asparagus, and salad. I introduce everyone and we chat while Pete and Kevin go back outside to check on the barbecue.

It turns out he's cooking steaks. I know he chose this meal on purpose, and it's romantic. As we sit at the dinner table, Pete feels the need to explain the reason for this meal, but also that he's been cooking it in different ways to see what tastes better. Barbecue was the winner.

"So, in my spare time, I've been doing this and Kaden's experiment," Pete says.

Be still, my heart. "You're really doing it?"

He shrugs like it's nothing when it really isn't nothing. "Yeah. I've got some serious jitters right now, but I've gotten a lot done with work, that's for sure."

This man is to-die-for incredible. He's busy with work and participating in Kaden's experiment, and working on his steak game.

Where has he been all my life?

"Yeah, Cece loves those pastries you suggested to her," Kevin chimes in. "Her bakers are experimenting with recipes right now. And you've been flying with their social media posts."

"The pastries were all Nichole's idea." He points his fork at me and winks.

"Oh. My. Lanta," Taryn interrupts through a mouthful of steak. "This is delicious! The only thing that's missing is whiskey."

Pete laughs as he gets up from the table and makes his way to a small bar in the corner of the dining room full of fancy wine glasses. He pulls out a short glass with Mount Rainier engraved on the side. "I knew you would say that, which is why I got this."

He pulls out a bottle of Laphroaig, and I swear I see Taryn drool.

"That's my favorite!" Kevin exclaims.

Taryn raises her hand across the table for a high five, which Kevin very enthusiastically accepts. Yup, that's going to be Taryn's man soon.

"I love you," she whispers to Pete.

"Well shoot, Felicia, you got competition!" Becca says to me with a laugh.

"Probably too much competition," Kacey mumbles, her eyes directed at Pete. His eyes harden as he glances back at her, like he's warning her to stop talking. I watch them for a few seconds, waiting for someone to break the silence, while also wondering what Kacey meant with that comment.

Kacey finally clears her throat. "Especially with the booze." She turns to me and says, "He's kind of a butt kisser. Likes to make sure he has everything he needs for whatever drink people want."

"You're the one that loves mojitos and asks for at least two every time you come over," Pete comments as he points to Kacey's glass. "Doesn't leave me much choice."

She sticks out her tongue. "It's free booze, dude. And I'm your sister." She motions to him, then to herself. "Older brother takes care of younger sister. It's in the Bible."

"I don't think it says exactly that," Becca comments with humor.

Kacey snarls playfully. "Well, it should. I'd benefit from it so much."

"Don't forget some of those bottles I brought over," Kevin says. "I deserve some credit."

I look at Sherri, who's silently observing with an amused expression, like she's used to this banter.

Kaden, Lucas, and Charlotte practically roll down the stairs and run into the front room with their guns. Lucas hops over the back of the couch and lands on the cushions, but bounces off and lands on the floor with a heavy *thud.*

"Lucas, you need to stop doing that!" Kacey shouts. "It doesn't make you look cool, and you get hurt every time!"

Lucas recovers quickly and completely ignores his mother before running to another part of the house. I don't even care that they're not eating with us, as long as they leave the adults alone and my son is smiling.

"Bruh, this whisky is life," Taryn says after taking a sip, then coughing slightly that makes everyone think she may have changed her mind. "And *really* smoky."

"I found a smoky marinade for the steak, so I thought that would be good." Pete passes the glass. "I've been looking for different marinades and watching YouTube videos on how to grill it. All thanks to my girl."

My girl. I think my bra just snapped off.

"So romantic," Becca says dryly through a mouthful of steak.

"Barf," Kacey jokes.

"Don't make me throw this asparagus at you," Pete warns.

"I guess I've never known you to be so . . . *freely* romantic," Kacey replies as she sips her mojito, a pointed look directed at Pete like they're sharing some inside joke. Again.

He smirks, then rolls his tongue over his teeth as if to contain whatever irritation he's feeling. This has happened twice now. What is Kacey talking about?

"Felicia has that effect on people," Becca interjects.

"Even with women?" Kacey smacks my arm playfully and I double over in laughter. "You got a secret you wanna share with us?" She lifts an eyebrow at Pete, who shakes his head and chuckles like it doesn't bother him, but somewhere in those glacial-blue eyes, her comments *are* bothering him.

"Nope, nope," I say in a high-pitched voice while I recover from laughing. "No secrets here."

But I start to wonder what secrets lay between her and Pete that I should know about.

Chapter 16

Pete

Freaking Kacey.

She can't stop herself from making insinuating comments in front of everyone. She's done it in front of Nichole twice now, and I got a tongue-lashing on top of it when we were at the movies.

"Your lack of honesty disturbs me," she had said.

I commended her for her *Star Wars* reference, but I told her to back off and let me deal with this. I know she loves and cares about me, but sometimes I wish she didn't love me so much.

The universe has a different plan. While I was barbecuing outside, Danny texted me.

Danny: Hey, Pete. Just wanted to tell you that I pitched the idea about you getting Anna an apartment, and she flat-out said no. Sounds like she doesn't mind going through a trial. If you wanna talk about other ideas to handle this, let me know.

Of course she turned it down. She wants revenge, and she wants it all in one piece. She can spend all the time she wants playing the victim, but I did the best I could as a husband.

I will figure this all out before Nichole ever finds out. That's my number one priority.

But right now, I'm enjoying drinks with my girlfriend and family. We've long since finished eating, we're abounding in cocktails and whiskey, and chatting with background music playing on the stereo in the front room. Kevin is showing considerable attention to Taryn, because now he's sitting next to her. She is particularly shy, as she's not adding much to the conversation, but she doesn't look like she wants him to leave her alone either. Well, good for them, I guess.

Becca freezes mid-sentence and gasps as she listens to the song playing on the stereo. One from ABBA.

"I love this song!" she shouts. "It makes me want to do an Irish step dance."

She doesn't wait for anyone's permission. She goes to the living room and starts doing the dance. And she's very bad at it. Laughably bad. She doesn't know which foot to step on and when to kick.

"Is that how it goes?" Nichole asks.

Becca scoffs. "I dunno. It just makes sense."

Nichole and Kacey eye each other, then join Becca, and they're both kicking at random intervals with no organization whatsoever. I just sit there and watch them, Nichole in particular. She's unapologetically silly, dancing and giggling hysterically.

I switch to a swing dancing song and join the party.

"Yes! Swing dancing!" Becca cheers. "I haven't done this in years!"

I hold out my hand to her. "Wanna dance?"

She takes my hand and we get right to spinning and rhythmic stepping. It's been years since I've done this, but I haven't forgotten what I learned when I used to go dancing in Seattle with a huge group of friends on Sunday nights.

When it ends, I play another swing song. I turn to Nichole and hold out my hand to her. "May I have this dance?"

She winces. "I dunno. I'm scared."

I wink. "I'll be gentle."

I pull her flush against my chest, my heart beating from exertion and simply having her close to me. I take both of her hands, then start doing the steps while swinging her arms side to side. She shrieks as she tries to follow along, then laughs harder when I spin her and she somehow spins in a whole different direction. Kacey and Becca stand to the side and make fun of her, but all in good fun.

Another song comes up, and I dance with her again. And again. And again.

I can't get enough of her.

And I never want anything to get in the way of that feeling.

After about an hour of endless dancing that eventually Kevin and Taryn join in on, everyone decides it's time to head out. Except Kacey, who tells everyone she's staying to help me clean up. She'd glowered at me when she said it; I know she's not just staying to help me.

I head back to the kitchen to do the dishes once everyone's left. Kacey steps up next to me to help, and she's saying absolutely nothing. Her expression is blank, but her aggressive dishwashing technique says something's brewing in her mind.

I brace my hands on the edge of the sink. Here we go. "What?"

She doesn't miss a beat. "You're going straight to Hell."

I sigh heavily and scrub the same plate I've already cleaned. "Yeah? And what's with all the hints you were dropping during dinner? It was like you were *trying* to throw me under the bus."

"I should have." She gets a cloth wet with soap. "It's not fair to her. You guys are *dating*. It's been some time now. It's not like you have a whole lot of options here."

I know she needs to know at some point. But there's no way I'm going to let my sister be the one to drop the bomb on her. "I'm not involving Nichole. She already has enough to deal with."

"Wow, you've opened a door and let in such crap." She turns to face me. "You're not worried about adding to her burden. You're worried that she'll break up with you." Now she's pointing a scolding finger at me. "Stop with the excuses and just tell her. It wouldn't be fair to her to be in this relationship without knowing that vital part of your life. It's not too late."

I don't know how many more times she plans on having this conversation, but it's getting old.

"Kace." I groan. I look her in the eye and state plainly, "I appreciate your concern. But I need to deal with this on my own."

Her lips form a tight line and she shakes her head in shame. "It's just . . . I've never seen you so happy. And I know she's happy too. I'd hate for this to fall apart because she finds out through another source." She gives me a relenting smile. "It'd be cool if she stuck around. You found a good one."

A corner of my mouth tilts up. "I did."

Kacey lays a wet hand on my shoulder. "Promise me you won't wait too much longer to tell her."

The way she looks at me with that pleading, begging expression hits me hard. She's desperate for this to be handled. Because she loves me.

Freaking sibling love.

"I promise," I say softly.

Satisfied, she returns to helping me with the dishes.

Kacey's wrong about one thing: I really am trying not to add to Nichole's problems. I also know without a doubt that she'll dump me if she finds out.

That will be the death of me.

Because I'm in love with her.

Chapter 17

Nichole

Steak and potatoes seem to be the main theme of our relationship now.

I invited Pete over for dinner tonight and that was my default idea. So here I am, preparing a feast for three while Kaden runs up and down the hallway asking when Pete's going to be here.

"I can't make him drive any faster, buddy," has become my go-to response.

"He said he'd bring Snickers ice cream!" he exclaims with the excitement of ten toddlers. "The best dessert the planet has ever seen!"

"I thought your favorite dessert was Oreos."

"That's my favorite cookie to prank you with," he replies with an evil grin.

"Well thanks for the reminder. I'm never buying Oreos again." I motion to the pan with the steaks in it as I move to the pot of boiling potatoes. "Flip those over for me."

"Like pancakes?"

"Whatever helps ya, kiddo."

It's just my luck that there's a knock on the door and Kaden forgets all about my request to flip the steaks. He darts for the door like whatever's behind it will save his life. "Yay, it's Pete!" he shouts.

"Hey, little man." Pete's voice warms my heart.

"Do you have the ice cream?" he asks.

I peer over from the kitchen where Pete hands him a plastic grocery bag. "That's really why you're excited to see me, right?"

Kaden takes the bag and looks inside like Pete might be lying. "No," he answers in a way that totally indicates he's lying. Kaden takes off down the hallway. He must've had something strong to drink if he thinks he can hide ice cream in his room.

"Dude, bring that back!" I call to him.

Pete busts out laughing when Kaden saunters back with his head down, like a sad dog.

"Don't gimme those puppy dog eyes, pal. It would melt by the time you got to it anyway."

"I have my ways of keeping things cold," he replies confidently as he puts the tub in the freezer.

Pete makes himself at home on the couch, arm draped over the back. He looks so . . . comfortable. Domesticated. Sitting there like he lives here, with that ever so slight smile on his face. Dark jeans and navy long-sleeved shirt paired with black utility boots. Suddenly, I'm wishing I could have him for dinner instead. "I didn't realize how obsessed you were over Snickers ice cream. Is that the only dessert you like?"

To my surprise, Kaden follows him to the living room. "No. I like Oreos."

I scoff, and it's loud. "You literally just told me you only like Oreos to prank me."

"That's just a good way to use them," he replies with a nonchalant shrug.

"Ohhhhh," Pete says in realization, "the toothpaste trick."

Kaden flinches in surprise. "How do you know about that?"

It's Pete's turn to scoff. "That's the oldest trick in the book. You should do the pencil on a quarter trick."

Kaden sits next to him, listening intently. I'm positive he doesn't pay this much attention in school. "What's that?"

Pete reaches in his pocket for a quarter, then searches my living room. "Do you have a pencil?"

I drop my jaw in playful shock. Then Kaden has the nerve to get up and find his backpack by the front door.

Brat.

"Are you really teaching my son how to prank me even more?"

"Oh, you're right. Sorry." He leans closer to Kaden when he comes back with the pencil, and whispers loudly to make sure I can hear him, "Try salt in her water next time."

"I heard that!" I shake my head and chuckle. "Dinner's ready, you freaks."

I portion out the food on three separate plates and stick a knife in the herb butter I made from scratch. Pete clears the table like the perfect gentleman he is. His parents taught him well.

"Here, I got you." He balances two plates on one arm and holds one plate on the other. "Kaden, bud, maybe you can help with the silverware?"

"Sure." Kaden goes right to help, pulling out forks and knives from the silverware drawer and following Pete to the dining room table. They look so natural, like this is routine for both of them. Kaden following him like an obedient pet is just plain adorable.

"Brings me back to my days as a clown," Pete tells us both like it's story time. "I'd juggle full plates without spilling a thing."

My eyes split wide open. "Seriously?"

He laughs uproariously as he sets everything down on the table. "No. I was a server at Applebee's for a while."

I rush from the kitchen to smack him on the arm multiple times. All it does is make him laugh harder.

"That was good," Kaden says, high-fiving Pete.

"You're both brats." I point to the chairs. "Sit and be happy."

I get drinks from the kitchen, and I see Pete nodding at the steak. "This is really good, hun."

Kaden winces as he takes a bite. My stomach falls. I hate making food my kid doesn't end up enjoying. "Doesn't taste like what we had at Pete's house," he comments in a disappointed tone.

Great. My kid doesn't like my cooking. I really hope that doesn't influence Pete's opinion.

"You know, not everyone can cook steak real good," Pete notes in the kindest tone possible as I'm bringing glasses of water back to the table. "Some people don't cook it long enough so it still looks raw, or they cook it too long so it's tough and gross. You might as well have chicken at that point, am I right?"

Kaden chuckles, and I'm waiting for Pete to get to the point. Did he just lie just to make me happy?

"But your mom did it perfectly," he says. "It may not taste the same as mine because there's more than one way to make it. But it works because it's still delicious." He motions to the herb butter. "Try it with that."

Kaden scoops some butter and spreads it on his steak. It's still hot, so it melts. He takes a bite. I get the privilege to watch his eyes go wide in excitement. "That's good!"

Pete winks. "I told you. She did a good job, didn't she?"

Kaden bobs his head. "Thanks, Mom!"

"Put the butter on the potatoes. It's mind-blowing."

This man is . . . incredible. He's not even a dad, but he just completely did a one-eighty on Kaden's opinion on dinner. And he made him show gratitude. He and I would work incredibly well together as parents.

I've died and gone to Heaven.

"If you eat it all, you can have an extra scoop of ice cream," I add.

That's when Kaden shovels it into his mouth like it's his last meal. Pete looks up at me and smiles. I mouth "thank you" while blushing intensely. I can't see it, but I definitely feel the heat rising in my cheeks.

"I'll get the ice cream!" Kaden shouts after he finishes his meal and races to the freezer.

"Do you need help cleaning up?" Pete asks, rising from the table and collecting plates.

"Nah. I'm good. You two have fun."

After they put the dishes in the sink, they serve up their ice cream, go in the living room to play *Fortnite*, and all I hear for the next half hour are gunshots and monster screams as I do the dishes.

I watch them closely the whole time. They're shouting excitedly, high-fiving each other and giving commands like the baristas do at Caffeinated Vino. True boys in their natural habitat.

Hours later, that transitions into trying to find a movie to watch, which took way too much time because we couldn't decide on something that wasn't *Star Wars* related. "I'm tired of *Star Wars*," Kaden whines, because he's a brat. We end up putting on the first *Transformers* movie because I love my kid and I would do anything for him.

We're all quiet until the part where Sam's parents burst into his room and find Megan Fox in there, a particularly funny scene. But I'm the only one laughing. Am I the only one who thinks this part is hilarious? Am I one of those people that laughs at things that aren't funny?

When I look next to me, I see what's going on.

The boys have fallen asleep. Pete's arm is slung around Kaden's shoulders and Kaden's head is resting on his chest.

Like the Grinch, my heart grows three sizes bigger. My child feels safe enough to fall asleep on him, and that means the world to me. He loves him.

I take out my phone and snap a photo of them sleeping and send it to my Felicias. It's sweet enough that I think I might make it my wallpaper. There's no photo more perfect than my two favorite men cuddled up together.

Becca: Okay, that's kind of adorable.

Me: Ikr?!

Taryn: Kaden cuddled up with your boyfriend? That should be in the Guinness World Records.

It really should be. Kaden is usually guarded with new people, but Pete walked into our lives and Kaden acted like he was his best friend, right from the get-go. I was guarded too, for both our sakes.

I don't have to be anymore. Pete is everything I've dreamed of, and then some.

Finally, I feel ready to admit the one thing to myself that I was afraid I would never feel again. The one thing I have never felt so sure of in my life.

I'm so in love with this man.

"I wanna show you something."

I came to clean Pete's house, but I can't focus on anything other than my gorgeous boyfriend.

He leads me to his garage, back to the table with the unfinished diorama. Next to the wooden box is an extensive list. That makes me smile.

Dad smoking a cigar.

Both my parents on their wedding day.

Nichole drinking coffee.

"What is this?"

Pete wraps his arm around my waist. "Ideas on what to do with Dad's unfinished project." He tilts his head down to look at me adoringly. "I started coming up with some ideas for things that would mean a lot to him if he saw it. Then I started thinking, maybe he'd want me to do something that meant something to *me*." He shrugs. "You gave me the push I needed to do something with it."

I lean my head on his chest while smiling widely. "I'm glad."

Keeping Pete as a client allows me to see him more often than if we were just dating. Like, a lot. But, the more I see him, the more chances I have to tell him I love him. And it's near impossible not to blurt it out right now. I want him to open the garage door so I can shout it to all the neighbors to the point where they start throwing stuff at me to shut me up.

"I should be productive today," I say through a contented sigh that says I do *not* want to be productive.

"You know—" he starts in a low voice, turning me to face him. His grip on my hips tightens. "It feels wrong to pay you."

My skin tingles with enough heat to burn off my clothes. His fingers find my belt loops and he pulls me flush against his solid, muscled chest. I get a whiff of charcoal and wood, and my God, it makes him irresistible.

My arms settle on his shoulders. He turns his head slightly to pepper my forearm with kisses, his beard caressing my skin.

"We might be dating, but it don't mean I don't need money."

Pete lets out a throaty chuckle. "Oh you play dirty."

He kisses me. My hands instinctively reach to the back of his head and I pull him closer, making him kiss harder. Then he lifts me by the legs and sets me on the table. Good God, it's hot that he's so strong.

"You're making this extremely difficult," I mumble between kisses. "I have another client and my skin is gonna be so chafed."

"I'm behind on work and you don't hear me complaining," he quips.

This is true, because this is the way it's been the last few weeks. I'll come clean his house, but spend more time making out while he puts off work and ignores all emails and phone calls. One time, we ended up in a coat closet at Kacey's house and we took down the whole rack. Coming up with a lie for that one made it all the more fun. We settled on the story of finding a mouse that we were trying to catch and release back outside. Kacey wasn't buying it, but the pleading look I was giving her made her drop the subject. Wise choice on her part.

"Okay, I really have to go." I give him one last kiss and hop off the table.

"I have to work. But I don't want to." His hands run up and down my arms. "You're too distracting."

"I'm sorry."

"Why? I'm not." He gives me one last peck on the lips before he relents. "Okay, go. I'll call you later."

"Okay." "I love you" is on the tip of my tongue, but I bite down hard, and I close the door.

Chapter 18

Nichole

"How do you get anything done if he's still your client?" Becca asks as she does the dishes long after dinner. She loves to cook, and I didn't want to tonight, so I gave the duty to her. Her offering to do the dishes was a godsend, because I can finally sit on my comfy couch.

My gaze roams the room before I shamefully answer, ". . . I don't."

Becca freezes, a sad look crossing her face, and I know exactly what she's thinking. She wants a relationship like mine, where we can't keep our hands off each other.

I wish I could convince her that it will happen for her someday.

"I don't think he's complaining." Taryn takes a shot of whiskey. "Get it, Felicia!"

"He's not." I giggle, so giddy and so in love. It's been a month since that moment in Pete's garage, and I'm about to explode. He still hasn't said he loves me, so instead of thinking about it too much, I focus on helping Kaden with his science fair project, or getting him together with Kacey's kids and have Oscar tag along. It's been a henhouse with all these kids, but it's a good distraction.

I rest my leg on Taryn's lap so she can rub my feet, but I forget that she finds feet absolutely disgusting until she shoves my leg off her and practically runs to the kitchen to get away.

"But it's so hard not to tell him I love him," I add.

"Yeah, but wait for him to say it," Becca says from the kitchen. "Just so you don't jump the gun and get your hopes up, ya know."

"There's no way he doesn't feel the same way," Taryn assures me.

"What if he never says it?"

Becca and Taryn exchange a wary glance. "Then that will tell you everything you wanna know," Taryn answers.

My stomach sinks. I love Pete with all my heart, but I didn't think about how it would feel if he didn't feel the same way. Maybe he's genuinely a good guy and he's just not there yet.

Crap. That's my doubt and lack of trust creeping in. I don't want that. Pete hasn't given me the slightest reason why I shouldn't trust him.

I just want him to say it.

As the evening settles, I leave my girlfriends in the living room to watch *The Angry Birds Movie* to say good night to Kaden, who's been hiding in his room most of the evening.

"Time for bed, kiddo," I say as soon as I open his door.

"Aw man," he complains while he continues to stare at the screen. "Five more minutes."

"Yeah, no. Five more minutes is two hours in Kaden language."

"I like my language, though." He grins widely, playing the innocent kid.

I put on my best stern-mom look. "You want me to put you to sleep with NyQuil?"

His face goes from amused to frightened, and I've never been prouder of my parenting skills. "Bedtime it is."

"Good boy."

He turns off the TV and shuffles under the covers. I turn on his blue lava lamp, the only thing that will help him sleep besides the glow-in-the-dark stars on the ceiling.

I shut the bedroom light off. "Sleep good baby. Love you."

"Wait. Mom?"

I stop just as I step into the hall. "Yeah?"

There's a short pause before he asks, "Are you and Pete getting married?"

Okay. Didn't expect a deep question like that. And now my brain is going a million miles a minute. I have no clue how to go about explaining this in a way he can accept without also lying through my teeth. Telling him no would disappoint him and think Pete would never officially be a part of our lives. Telling him yes is jumping the gun on a conversation I haven't even had with Pete yet, all while getting his hopes up.

I blame Jared for putting me in this position. Stupid man with one thing on his mind.

But I digress.

I have to settle for an answer somewhere in the middle. "I don't know yet."

"I think it would be cool."

My heart leaps to my throat. I close the door and sit on the edge of his bed. "Yeah? You like Pete?"

The bed jiggles as he nods excitedly with a wide smile. Something about that small gesture of approval gives me hope. Maybe Pete is the end of my journey as a single mom. Maybe he can be the dad Kaden needs. That's all to say, if Pete wouldn't mind being married to me.

"Good." I lean forward to kiss his forehead. "I like Pete too."

I bid him good night one more time. I stand outside his door, then softly lean against it to recoup from what just happened.

Kaden likes Pete.

Kaden wants me to marry Pete.

Kaden approves of me sharing my love between them.

How would Pete feel if he knew about this? Would he freak out? Would he tell me we need to slow down? Would he say he never actually wanted to be a stepparent?

Oh man. All questions that will prevent me from sleeping tonight.

Chapter 19

Pete

"You've been quiet. What's going on?"

Every single time I've been on a date with Nichole, she's always expressive. She's always silly without a care in the world. She always has a way of talking to people.

We've been at Caffeinated Vino for about ten minutes and she's barely said a word. I've suffered through the silence by taking in the New Year's decor stuck to the windows and fake snowflakes hanging from the strings of fairy lights.

Life experience is enough to tell me that if a woman is quiet, something is wrong. Or they're thinking deeply about something. But Nichole always tells me what she was thinking about.

She sighs. "I don't want you to feel pressured in any way when I tell you."

I take her hand and kiss it. "I won't. Just tell me."

She traces her thumb back and forth on my skin. Her palms are sweaty, which makes me a little wary. I take a sip of my drink as she says, "So, last night, Kaden kinda threw me for a loop."

"Yeah? What happened?"

She releases a nervous sigh. "He asked if you and I were getting married."

I nearly choke on my coffee. No wonder she was worried about broaching this subject. This is a huge deal. She's talking about *marriage*.

Do I want that with her? Absolutely. Am I able to do that right now? That's another story. A story that requires me to finally tell her the truth. Which is also why I haven't told her I love her.

"Ugh, I knew that would freak you out."

I clear my throat while vigorously shaking my head. "I'm not freaked out, hun. Just surprised." I take her hand again to let her know I'm open to talking this through. "What did you tell him?"

She glances around the shop until her eyes land on the streetlights shining outside in Landing Plaza. The weather is surprisingly mild, although very wet, as Washington always is in December. "Maybe we should take a walk?"

Oh boy. This is serious.

The situation with Anna hasn't changed much. I ignore her calls because I already know what she's going to say. I ignore Danny's calls because he wants a different answer other than the one I've given him the last six months, and that answer is the same. I don't want a trial, and we haven't found a solid compromise. Dating Nichole hasn't changed my resolve to prove a point to Anna. If anything, it's strengthened it. Six months is a long time to drag this out. Her boyfriend hasn't found a way to move out of his mother's house. That has to drive her crazy. She'll back down. Once she does, I won't have to worry about telling Nichole anything.

We walk through Landing Plaza with our warm paper cups in our hands. I look inside a restaurant that makes wood-fired pizza as I wait for Nichole to find the words for this conversation. "I just told him I didn't know," she finally answers, taking a sip to break the silence. She cringes at me once she swallows. "I also told him I wasn't opposed to it."

Neither am I. If I were able to, I'd drop to one knee in the middle of the sidewalk and pop the question.

It's everything I've ever wanted. *She's* everything I've ever wanted. She comes as a package with her son, the coolest kid I've ever met. Besides Lucas, he's the only kid I've genuinely connected with. None of it was forced, and he actually looks forward to seeing me when I come over. That speaks volumes for someone who never planned on being a father.

I'd do it in a heartbeat for Nichole and Kaden. I'd do anything for them.

"Well, I don't know if this helps," I begin. "I hope you know by now that I love Kaden. He's a great kid."

Nichole says nothing. Little does she know I'm not finished. I've held back long enough. She deserves to know what I feel.

"I would take on the father role if it means being with you."

She stops dead on the sidewalk, and I move in front of her to grab her shoulders and look into her eyes. She inhales shakily and smiles ear to ear, on the verge of tears. Or laughter. Or both.

"I've known since the day I met you that I wanted you and everything you come with." I get choked up when I prepare for what I want to say next. I've only said it to one person in my whole life. It's scary to say it to someone else, but also thrilling, because nothing has ever been truer. "I love you, Nichole."

She releases a choked sob, letting the tears fall. "I love you too, Pete."

She takes my face and kisses me with her tearstained cheeks against the softness of my beard. I've never known joy like this, to be in a healthy relationship with someone who's never hidden her true self, who's never given me an inkling of something wrong. It's beyond difficult to put that happiness into words when I kiss her back with everything I have. She has my whole heart to do as she wishes.

"I should've said, 'I know,'" she says through a quivering voice.

"Oh you're right. I'm sorry. Let's start over." I clear my throat and put on my best high-pitched voice to imitate Princess Leia. "I love you."

Nichole lowers her chin as she prepares to speak in a manly voice, and I snort. "Stop, you're distracting me!" she says as she gets into her role. "Wait, let's move over here."

She takes my hand and pulls me to a nearby roundabout, right across from the movie theater, with a large structure with intertwined strips of hammered metal, all curved to form a globe. The inside of the globe has a bubbling water fountain to add to the fancy ambience.

I'm placed in front of her, close to the water fountain, where the sound of her throat clearing blends with the rushing water. "I know," she answers through the deepest voice she can muster.

I fully laugh at her attempt, and kiss her smile and all the joy she emanates. I can never tire of those lips. They're all I think about anymore, including that gorgeous smile.

I've got it bad.

I love this woman.

Which is why I'm going to tell her everything on our next date.

Chapter 20

Nichole

Life is perfect. Everything is wonderful.

I love Pete.

Pete loves me.

Pete loves my kid.

Pete doesn't mind being a stepparent.

Becca was right. God really did say "hold my beer" and surprised the crap out of me. He put me on cloud nine and I'm not coming down.

My heart wanted to burst from my chest when I told Pete what Kaden said. My nerves were all over the place, but Becca told me how to start off the conversation, and his calm disposition made it easier for me to say it. Telling him I wasn't opposed to marriage was a giant leap for me, but I had a right to know how he felt, based on the opinions of my Felicias. I didn't expect it to lead into him proclaiming his love for me too, but it went so smoothly. It came up at the best time, and it was freeing to get it off my chest.

It has to be a dream. I'm worried I'll wake up tomorrow only for it to be a fantasy. I've had a few of those. I've dreamt of telling Pedro Pascal that I love him and he became my husband, only to find it wasn't real. I felt so lucky to marry a famous person, only for that to disappear the second I woke up. I've tried to force myself to fall back asleep to return to that dream, but it never works.

Thank God I don't have to do that anymore. I just have to wake up and remind myself it was all real.

Pete drops me off at my fourplex, the blue spaceship lights in his car making us look like those Avatar characters. It's surreal, just like this moment.

He leans over the console to kiss me. "I love you."

"I love you too."

He waits for me to approach my building, the outdoor lights of Camilla's and my apartments shining bright enough to help me find the doorknob for my key.

And a note taped to my door.

I have to stare at it for a solid minute, because I can't tell if someone's screwing with me, or if it's true. I don't recognize the handwriting either. I know it's not Jared. He doesn't ever plan on coming back to Washington. Even if he did, there's no reason for him to leave a note like this on my door. He doesn't even know what's going on in my life.

There's way too much happening. One thing at a time. This is the best night of my life. I'm riding that high for a while.

I take the note and walk into the apartment. The TV and living room lights are on and Kaden's door is closed. My babysitters did a good job.

"Sooooo, how did it go?" Becca asks as Taryn lowers the volume on the TV.

Oh. Right. My date. That's more important than this note.

I flap my arms at my sides, trying to contain my excitement. "He said he loves me."

Both of my Felicias squeal quietly to avoid waking Kaden up, and clap for me, leaping from the couch to give me a hug. We all jump at the same time in a circle, giggling our hearts out. Moments like these, where I can share relationship milestones with my friends, is everything to me.

Taryn points at the paper in my hand. "What's that?"

"I found this on my door." I hand them the note.

"Holy crap," Becca mutters under her breath. "This is . . . bad."

"I really, really hope this isn't true," Taryn says. "I mean, it can't be. I would think he would've disclosed this by now."

"Who do you think left it?"

"I have no idea," Becca says. "I didn't hear a knock on the door at all tonight."

"People don't usually knock on the door to leave a note," Taryn points out. "It's been quiet tonight, though."

"Wouldn't surprise me if it's a stupid prank," Becca notes. "You could still ask Pete anyway, just to be safe. It doesn't seem like he's left out any pertinent details of his life at this point."

"Then what is this person's motive for leaving this?" My throat pulses in a panic that I have to swallow down hard. There's no way that Pete is hiding anything from me.

What if on the off chance that this is the exception?

"Guys, what if I've fallen for another trap?" I ask despondently.

"If it is, he's due for a butt whuppin'." Taryn emphasizes with her pointer finger.

So, there may be some truth here. Someone must've taken an opportunity to screw over Pete, and drag me down with him. That takes a vindictive, bitter person.

There's only one person in Pete's life I can think of that would want to destroy his life.

His ex.

I've seen a lot of romance movies and TV shows. There's always an angry lover thirsty for revenge, and they usually have something in their arsenal to use to destroy their ex. Every single time, that little fact, that little lie, is true, and it makes everything fall apart.

God. I can't believe I'm referring to movie plots as a guiding point here. It can still be valid, though.

My rising from the couch back to the door says yes. "I need some answers, and I need them now."

"We'd totally go with you if it wasn't illegal to leave a child home alone." Becca feels the need to inform me.

"He'd be fine if one of us stays, but if you go, I go too," Taryn insists.

Becca turns and grabs my shoulder. "Keep us posted."

It's all a blur when I jog to my car, still in my date clothes, then go way past the speed limit for the seven minutes it takes to get to Pete's house. It normally takes ten, but I'm a little desperate. Maybe I should've had a shot of Taryn's whiskey before I left.

I let nothing hold my car back from rolling full speed downhill to Pete's house. I may have run over a squirrel. *Sorry, buddy.*

I slam on the brakes in front of his driveway and leave the engine running while I run up the steps and pound incessantly on his door. Nothing happens for a few seconds, and I start to doubt that he can hear me.

He has a security camera. He must know someone is here, and that someone is losing her freaking mind.

The sides of my palms and wrists start to turn red and painful when he finally swings the door open. I stumble forward at first, as I didn't even hear him approaching the door and I wasn't going to stop till he opened.

"Nichole?" His eyebrows crease in deep worry. "What's going on, hun? Are you okay?"

He has some nerve calling me "hun" if this note is true. I don't even have the answers, yet I'm already preparing for an attack. Because deep down, I believe there's some merit.

I hold up the note to his face. "Tell me this isn't true."

Chapter 21

Pete

Pete Daley is still married. Ask him why.

It takes all the self-control in my body to not crumple the sticky note or tear it into a million itty-bitty pieces.

Because I know Anna was the one who wrote this note. I'm not sure how she found Nichole's apartment, but that doesn't matter. This crosses the line.

She's so desperate to win in this divorce that she went so far as to track down Nichole and leave this life-altering news. Of course she found the one thing that means the world to me and felt the need to destroy it. She's like Lando in *Empire Strikes Back*, turning on his friends by opening the door, and there's Vader.

"I can't believe this," I whisper, shaking my head.

"So it's true?" Nichole's voice quivers and grows in volume. I'm screwed.

"Just in the legal sense, I swear." A weak defense for an argument where I'm in the wrong.

"And you didn't think to tell me when we started dating?" Her shouts echo into the street. I've never seen her so angry. I hate myself for being the reason for it. "I've been dating a married man!"

"I don't love her. I haven't for a while." All the defenses I want to make collide in my mind and I can't figure out which ones to say to her. "We've been done for months, I promise. She's bitter and resentful a-and she's been living with her boyfriend the last six months." I'm blabbering, but I'm trying to pick strong justifications for my stupidity.

Nichole flails her arms wildly. "Then why did you hide this from me?"

I start from the first of the list of reasons I told myself for months. "I didn't want to drag you into my problems. You're a single mom—"

She leans her face close to mine, a finger stabbing my chest. Okay, wrong thing to say. "Don't you *dare* throw that in my face! I may be a single mom, but that doesn't mean I don't deserve the truth from the man I'm dating. You had so many chances—*months*, actually—to tell me!"

"Because this is *my* problem to fix—"

"That's a cop-out and you know it! There is *no* excuse for this. *None*."

I stay silent. I have nothing to back up that statement, because it's the truth. The cold, God's honest truth.

In the back of my mind, I expected this. But I never expected to meet a woman so soon after separating from Anna. I was so sure Anna would eventually give in. Instead, she fought harder.

"Nichole." I grab her shoulders so she doesn't run away from me. "I'm sorry. I'm so, so sorry. I was just trying to take care of it myself without you feeling burdened. But that is *not* a statement about how I feel about you. If you take anything from this, just know it was not meant to make you feel like I don't respect you, because I do. You're the most amazing woman I've ever met, and my life has been incredible because you're in it. I was going to tell you the next time I saw you because you deserve to know. Because I love you. I love you so much, Nichole."

Tears collect in her eyes, and she shakes her head as she moves her gaze away from me. My heart sinks deeper into my stomach. I'm losing her. I can hold her arms tighter, but it won't stop her from slipping away from me.

"Everything else I told you was true. *Everything.* I may have left that detail out, but I gave you my all, and I will still give everything I have to be with you."

Her voice is weak, shaky, and wounded. "I opened up to you. I told you how much I struggled trusting men after all I've been through." She sniffles, her face a blubbery mess that I just want to kiss away. "But you made a fool of me instead. What's next? I find out Kacey isn't your sister? That your dad never died?"

That one hurts. I opened up to her about that, and I never pour my heart out that way to just anyone. "I would *never* lie about that."

"Well, how do you expect me to believe that you've told the truth about anything else?" A couple choked sobs escape her lips. "I've fallen in love with someone I don't know. My gut told me not to trust you, and I should have listened." She backs away, holding up her hands. "I'm done. We're done."

She runs down the steps. Away from me. Away from our friendship. Away from everything we ever shared.

"Nichole!" I chase after her, barefoot on the freezing-cold, wet concrete. "Nichole!"

She's already gotten in her car and peeled out of the driveway. She drives like she can't get away from me fast enough, which hurts worse. I watch her car soar uphill to the stop sign, getting smaller and smaller, like the likelihood of being able to fix this.

I trudge back up the steps to the front door, leaning against it as I close it. Everything happened the way I was afraid of. She found out, she broke up with me, and it's tearing me apart.

I slide down to the floor and cry. All the fury, all the pain, all the loss. I cry the hardest I have since Dad died.

I hate Anna. I hate myself. I hate reality. I hate that I did this. I hate that I put myself through this heartache. I hate my ego that encouraged me to make stupid decisions that destroyed everything that meant the most to me.

I have no one else to turn to for help. I've been rejecting it for so long—particularly from Kacey—because I thought I knew what was best. I wanted to deal with it on my own. I never should've lived that way, because right now, I need her support. Somehow, I find the strength to call her.

"Peter Pan! What's going on?" she answers with an energy I wish were contagious.

"Hey."

"Uh-oh. Are you okay? What happened? This isn't another prank, is it?"

"No. Can you come over?"

"Well shoot. Lemme put the kids to bed and I'll be over. Hang tight, big bro."

At this point, I'm hanging on by a thread. I'd rather go to sleep and wake up to a time when I never knew Anna, and Dad is still with us.

Kacey makes it to my house at lightspeed. Ten minutes is record time for her, especially when she had to put her kids to bed first. Something I appreciate about her. All speeding laws are moot when Kacey has an emergency.

All manners fly out the window, too, when she barges into my house without knocking. My grief-stricken body tumbles forward limply onto the floor as she shoves the door open, and I don't move. I don't care about anything.

"Dude, what's going on with you?" she snaps, then sees my tearstained face as I recover. "Oh. She knows."

I right myself and lean my head back against the door. "It's over. She's done."

She sighs heavily. I don't bother looking directly at her, because I already know what her expression will read, and right now is the worst time for her to say what she wants to say.

"Aw, you numbnuts," she says with compassion, and sits with me on the floor. "Look, as badly as I want to say I told you so and rub it in your face that I was right—which, I was—" I roll my eyes. "—I'm here for you."

"Thanks."

She rests her head on my shoulder and loops her arms around mine. Today felt like a glorious dream, knowing that Nichole loved me and I felt the same way ten times over.

Then it did a complete flip and I'm in the middle of my worst nightmare come to life—what Nichole would do once she knew the truth.

"Life is gonna suck," Kacey says in warning. Going through an impending divorce is reminder enough.

I lean my head into hers. "I know. I miss her already."

Kacey lifts her head. "Do you remember that guy I dated in high school? Brandon?"

I roll my eyes. That guy was a cocky, conceited dude who thought the whole world loved him. "Yes," I say in disgust.

"Do you remember how we broke up?"

I rear back to look at her. "I just know it sucked."

"That's an understatement." She turns to face me, excited to tell this story. "He told me his parents wanted him to avoid dating so he could focus on getting his grades up." She scoffs. "He was a completely different person. Basically kicked me to the curb. Avoided me like the plague. Didn't even look in my direction." She picks at her fingers, swallowing hard. "Then I caught him with another girl behind the bleachers just a week after he dumped me."

I remember that now. I was already in college, but I was willing to drive home to beat him up. *Nobody* hurts my sister.

"I was devastated. I wanted to die." She gesticulates. "Like, I legit didn't think I'd ever get through it. I'd be in this state of heartbreak curled up in a ball in the corner of my room. But I had school, you know. Couldn't just skip 'cause of a broken heart. So, I went to school. Took each day one at a time. Again. And again. And again. Until eventually, it didn't hurt so much." She snorts. "Especially when I put a laxative in his lunch."

I manage to smile at that. “You did?”

She giggles. “He was an upside-down volcano. It was wonderful.”

I laugh softly, because that’s all I can muster. I never knew she did that, but I wouldn’t have put it past her. She is my unfiltered sister, after all.

“I’m only telling you because you’re going to feel like you’ll never get through this, or it’ll hurt for the rest of your life. But if you just keep your head down and plow through each day, it won’t feel as painful. Time heals.”

I blow a raspberry. “I dunno if I’ll ever heal from this one.”

She lays her head on my shoulder again. “You will. I promise.”

Chapter 22

Nichole

Pete: Please call me back and let me explain.

Pete: I love you so much. That hasn't changed, and it never will. Can you please hear me out?

Pete: Hun, just tell me what you want. If you need space, I'll leave you alone, but you gotta say something. Please, I'm begging you.

That's just a few of the fifty-five other messages Pete sent since last night.

Last. Night.

I'm not ready to talk to him. Maybe I'll never be ready. I thought my silence was enough, but he's not accepting that. He wants to *explain*. Explain what? There's nothing to say!

I was too upset to even tell my girls what happened. In fact, I walked in huffing and puffing and went straight to my room. They got the point.

I don't even have the strength to get out of bed. I canceled all my cleaning jobs today. I had Kaden ask Camilla for a ride to school, and that was the extent of my parenting duties for the day. The rest of my energy is focused on how to stop crying.

That's right, I've been crying all night. My eyes are redder than Darth Maul and I'm sure I could scare Casper the Ghost. I can't even look at myself in the mirror without being terrified of what I look like.

Around noon, when my body wakes up from death, I roll over to grab my phone and send a text to my Felicias.

Me: emergency meeting at Caffeinated Vino. Tonight. Get comfy, this is gonna take a while.

Becca: Lemme caffeine it up and I'll be down.

Taryn: I gotchu, Felicia. Becks, we may have to get some shovels.

Becca: For what?

Taryn: To beat up a hoe and bury the evidence.

Becca: I'm down. Let the hoe-beatin' commence!

Even at rock bottom, they can make me chuckle. I know they got my back.

Pete: I hope you slept ok. Despite all this, I still love you. I hope you don't doubt that.

He hopes I don't doubt that? He can't be serious. I doubt literally everything now.

Pete: I won't stop texting till I get a response from you, Nichole.

Good Lord, the texts won't stop coming.

I turn off my phone and roll back over. Love sucks, and I don't want to deal with it right now.

"But, *why* is he still married?" Taryn asks after I tell them the whole story. She drags a tortilla chip through the spinach artichoke dip. "That's what's killing me. He obviously doesn't love her. And it's not like he's broke and can't afford a divorce. Those are usually the two biggest reasons people stay married."

I stare blankly at my mojito while stirring it, watching the mint leaves swirl in the liquid, and listening to the lo-fi music playing in the background. I don't know what to think, to be honest. I still haven't figured out how to tell Kaden that we broke up, because the thought of doing that makes me want to vomit. I can't break his little heart like that.

"Or he's trying to prove a point to his ex," Becca mumbles.

I narrow my eyebrows at her. "What do you mean?"

She swallows her Baileys and coffee. "Look, I'm not gonna be one to judge this situation because I don't have all the information. There's always another side to the story." She gives me a pointed look. "In my experience, ninety-nine point nine percent of the time, a guy's reason for acting a certain way is extremely stupid. *However*, I have a gut feeling that Pete is the point one percent of the minority that actually has a valid explanation."

Taryn nods after sipping her whiskey sour. "Normally, I'd have a different opinion, but Felicia here has a point. Pete just doesn't seem like the dishonest type, and I don't think he's a bad person." She gives me a stern look with a finger pointed at me. "And you know I read people well."

"So." My voice comes out quiet and worn down. "What are you saying I should do?"

Becca's face crinkles with what she's about to say, as if she doesn't think I'll take it well. "I think you need to hear him out."

"Uninterrupted," Taryn adds firmly. "People make mistakes. So let him explain the reasons for his."

I gasp, my arms flopping onto the table. I don't, in fact, like this advice. "The guy lied to me! What is there to say?"

"But don't you think it's worth getting the full story before deciding to cut him loose?" Taryn asks, pausing to let me think about that. "All you know is that he's still legally married. Nothing else. If the tables were turned, wouldn't you want the chance to give the full story?"

Crap. She's right. There's nothing worse than feeling denied an explanation because they're too pissed off to hear it.

"Fine," I reply, clipped. "I'll text him." I grab my phone from my purse that has been turned off all day. "But after this, I'm done with men," I say with my teeth clenched.

"You won't be, but okay," Becca says with an eye roll.

"Well, at least promise us you'll let him get a word in," Taryn says. "And if it still doesn't work out, *then* you can swear off men."

"Then you can join me in the single forever club!" Becca exclaims with excitement that is so fake. "Because Felicia over there has been talking to Pete's friend Kevin."

I muster a small smile. "You got Kevin's number?"

Taryn shrugs like it's nothing. "Just talking. Nothing's happening really."

Becca cups a hand around her mouth so Taryn doesn't see. "She's downplaying it," she whispers.

As they argue about Taryn's relationship status, I text Pete begrudgingly.

Me: Fine. Can you meet me at CV?

If this conversation goes haywire, then I won't have a choice but to give up on all mankind. But hey, at least I'll always have my girls. And Kaden.

The speed in which he texts back is lightning fast. Like a puppy dog waiting for its owner. Kind of endearing.

Wait. No. NO! Bad Nichole. He's the naughty one!

Pete: I'll be there in ten.

"Pete's coming in a few minutes," I grumble.

"Oh? He's coming here?" Becca asks in surprise. "Well, I need to pretend to have plans after this then."

"I'll just text Knox," Taryn says. "If all else fails, we can hang out with him and Katie. Maybe Kevin too."

"Because I *so* wanna be the fifth wheel," Becca replies dryly.

Taryn gives her a pointed look. "What else you gonna do? Sit at home with your brother and cat?"

She leans into Taryn's shoulder. "I will always pick cuddling with my cat over being a fifth wheel on a date. Just toss me a good book and I'm set."

Taryn shrugs and continues to text Knox, just as I see Pete walking in. Man, he got here fast. Did he somehow develop lightspeed capabilities since last night?

"Hey, Pete!" Becca greets him way too loudly, waving erratically. She gets up and gives him the most awkward hug when he approaches our table. Even Becca knows she's being weird, but she can't seem to stop herself. "How's it going?"

Facepalm. *Stop talking, Becca.*

Pete chuckles hesitantly, clearing his throat. "Um, doing okay."

Becca nods. "Good. Good."

Taryn smacks her arm. "Felicia, Knox is waiting for us."

Becca looks ultra confused. "I don't have plans with Knox."

Taryn grips her elbow and drags her away from us. "You do now."

Thank God for Taryn.

Knox walks in to meet the girls, and they make a quick exit. I can barely look Pete in the eye, even though I know he's standing right next to the booth.

"Hey," he says thickly.

"Hey."

He sits across from me, fisting his hands together on the table. I still avert my gaze, staring at the drink in my hand that's definitely too diluted to drink now. "I know I've been bombarding you, but I really, really want to explain everything." He sighs. "If you still choose not to be with me after I tell you, I understand, but please just give me a few minutes of your time."

Well, I have to give him credit for giving me a choice in the matter with no hurt feelings. "Fine."

He sighs again, nervously this time, and takes a moment to choose his words. My focus is hard-set on the wood of the table, just waiting.

"When Anna and I were married," he starts, "I gave her everything she wanted. I just wanted to be a good husband. Happy wife, happy life, right?" He chuckles bitterly. "Things were fine for a while. Anna didn't like how much time I spent with Dad in the garage. But I didn't see the big deal. This was my dad." He swallows hard. "When he died, he put in the will to give us the house and had Mom move in with Kacey so she would never be alone. When I needed support, Anna felt I was neglecting her when she needed attention. I was having a really hard time just getting through each day." His lips twitch uneasily. "Apparently, she was feeling so neglected that she found someone else to give her what she wanted. I was so furious that I kicked her out without giving her a chance to pack anything."

I already heard this part. Still waiting for the part where I understand everything else.

"She moved in with her boyfriend, and little did she know that he actually lived in his mother's basement. I got a lawyer, got the divorce papers, and sent them to her to sign. What I didn't expect her to do was use this as leverage. Because

I didn't allow her to come back and get her stuff, and that I wasn't being an attentive husband, she thought she could punish me." He swallows, and I'm slightly scared of what he's going to finish his thought with. "She will only sign the papers if I give her the house."

I knew this woman was vindictive and spoiled, but my God, she's going above and beyond.

"So, why didn't you just give her the house?" I ask quietly.

I take a moment to finally peek at his facial expression. He winces at my question, wringing his hands anxiously. "Nichole, this is my parents' house. It still holds everything that belonged to Dad. There's no way I can give that to her and her boyfriend. They will never appreciate it the way I do. So I took this opportunity to show her she'll never control my relationship with my father. That she could've been more understanding. I just . . ." He gestures strongly with his hands, yet finishes in a defeated tone. "I wanted to prove a point because I thought Dad would've wanted me to."

Man. Becca was right. Usually men have stupid excuses for doing what they do, but Pete's . . . actually make sense. However, dragging out this divorce hasn't proved anything, and it doesn't excuse him lying to me for *months*. I trusted him with my insecurities, everything that I was afraid of. Which were perfect times for him to tell me what was going on.

He's handled this entire situation awfully.

"Sooooo why didn't you tell me any of this?"

Pete leans forward, earnestly pleading. "Believe me, I was going to tell you everything on our next date. I was tired of holding back and I felt you needed to know it all. Then Anna left that note and ruined it."

I swear my heart stops and I'm not breathing. "*Anna* left that note?"

"I knew from the handwriting."

I'm positive my brain's wires just snapped. She wanted to get back at him so badly that she went so far as to find my house? The woman will stop at nothing.

Why do all the great guys end up with crazy women?

"Well, now I need to move," I utter before sipping the diluted mojito.

Pete waves a dismissive hand. "No, don't worry about that." He goes back to earnest pleading. "It sounds stupid, but I was afraid you wouldn't date me if you knew. And I didn't want to wait till the divorce was final to ask you out because you were just so amazing and beautiful and funny, and I felt like you'd be snatched up before I had my chance."

Ugh. So he was impatient and impulsive. I should be flattered that he thought someone else would snatch me before he had a chance—even though we all know that wasn't going to happen—but it isn't enough to forgive him for months of deceit.

"You've been holding out because of some male ego thing you have going on?"

Pete hangs his head shamefully for a moment, then lifts it to say, "I simply don't want her to win. But, I don't care about it anymore. I just want to make this right with you." If he could lean across the table any more, he'd be on his knees right now. "I'll give her the house and move in with Kacey."

Things he could have decided to do last night. Heck, he could have done all of that in the first place, and we wouldn't be having this conversation.

"You're only saying that because the secret's out now. How do I know you even want to save this relationship? How do I know you don't love her anymore?"

Pete sighs harsher this time, holding back words of frustration he has no right to have, but he corrects himself. "I can't emphasize this enough: I feel nothing for her. *Nothing.* I've been calling her the Antichrist for a reason."

I chuckle, but it's empty. No smile. No humor. In any other circumstance, I'd be laughing harder. But it's not enough to not be mad at him anymore.

"Nichole, say something," Pete pleads softly, grasping for my free hand while my other one is holding my head up by the temple. As much sense as his story makes, it's a lot to process. None of it takes away the pain he's caused me.

Between the two hands of different emotions, only one weighs the most. I jerk my hand away from his.

"Pete, as much as I love you . . ." I swallow through the tightness in my throat. "I still have a hard time trusting you."

His face falls, devastated and heartbroken. Exactly what I felt when I found everything out.

"You clearly have things to deal with, so it's best if we go our separate ways until you can get everything figured out." I tap a fingernail on the table several times, trying to drive my point home, and rise to leave. "And it's best that you're no longer my client."

"Yeah," he replies gravely, tears trickling down to his beard. I've never seen him cry, and it's breaking my heart seeing him this way. "I understand."

I have to walk away, no matter how hard this is. I have to keep my self-respect intact, even if he's the most perfect man I've ever known.

"Before you go." Pete reaches into his jeans pocket and hands me a folded sheet of paper. "Please give this to Kaden for me."

That poor kid is going to be devastated without Pete in our lives. That's going to be a whole other problem to figure out.

"I will. Bye, Pete." I turn and practically run for the doors so I don't have to watch him cry. It's only making *me* want to cry.

I have to walk away. I *have* to. No matter how many times I tell myself that, it doesn't feel like I've made the right choice. Maybe I should have just forgiven him. Forget the whole thing and start over.

No. I'm not stooping so low that I'll date a married man. All the movies about love affairs say the same thing—they will never leave their spouse, no matter how many times they tell their partner they will.

Pete says he's going to give up the house. Doesn't mean he actually will. That house means everything to him. He still has to prove he's a *man*.

What a load of crap.

I wait to get in my car before I open the paper. I expected it to be some drawing, or a goodbye letter, or a receipt for a virtual *Fortnite* experience I didn't know existed. Turns out, it's none of those things.

There're dates, times, amounts of coffee, different brands of energy drinks, and detailed notes.

His results for Kaden's science fair project.

Despite everything, he loved Kaden enough to do this for him.

I cry harder than I ever have in my life.

Chapter 23

Pete

I hadn't realized just how much breakups suck.

The last month has dragged so slowly. I'm talking, like, iceberg slow. I don't remember the last time I had a good night's sleep. I don't remember the last time I had a healthy meal. I sure don't remember the last time I wore anything other than my Darth Vader robe. I probably stink. I wouldn't know.

With Nichole no longer my house cleaner, my bedroom is a tumultuous disaster. Clothes are all over the floor; the bathroom is covered in beard clippings, soap scum, and dust; and the curtains messily draped over my windows turn my room into an abyss of darkness. Which reminds me, the reflection in my mirror is telling me my beard is getting long and rough. I haven't used my beard oil in a while.

No reason for me to care. Nichole's not going to be around to see or feel it. I haven't talked to her since we met at Caffeinated Vino. I don't even know what she thought of my results for Kaden's science fair project.

Everything in my brain is telling me I need to log in to my computer and get to work, but I feel like torturing myself instead. I go into my upstairs office, where all my *Star Wars* collections belong, and reminisce. The second time Nichole came to clean, she was so nervous about knocking over my precious items and breaking them, she was a sweaty mess the whole time.

I trudge downstairs to the foyer. The first time Nichole came over, she was a stressed out, sweaty mess with a pimple on her forehead, and she got lost finding my house. Now I'll never see her on the other side of it.

The kitchen. I made Nichole coffee to calm her down, and she raved over my caramel macchiato. Now the sink is piled with dishes and dried food all over it.

The hall closet. Which brings me back to making out with Nichole at Kacey's in secret and lying to her about what happened to the rack. Not that she fell for it.

She's the woman who made me happiest. The woman who made me forget everything that was wrong in my life. Now I can't open it without thinking of her taking down the coatrack.

Everything just feels wrong. I wasn't this torn up when Anna left me. If anything, it was kind of a relief. Sure, I was brokenhearted because everything we built was destroyed, but that was the extent of it. Now it's like my heart is splattered all over the floor, and there's no hope left.

"Pete? You alive in here?"

Kacey's been coming over frequently to check on me. She ends up cleaning my kitchen, which I've tried telling her not to do, but she gives me a look that tells me there will be hell to pay if I keep arguing with her. "I'm a mom. I clean up on autopilot," she told me once. But there's no way I'm letting her into my bedroom to deal with *that* mess.

"Yeah," I respond, lifeless and lazy.

She walks into my tornado of a kitchen and takes a minute to examine my hobo-like self. "Dude. Have you heard of a shower?" She crinkles her nose. "It smells like shriveled-up balls in here."

I don't even have the heart to laugh. "Do I even wanna know how you know what that smells like?"

Kacey shakes her head vigorously. "Petey, you've got to get yourself together. You still have so much to do for the launch at Caffeinated Vino. You're not gonna get anything done if you keep procrastinating."

I still have to make more social media posts, send emails to newsletter subscribers, create the event page, take photos of the finished products, and maintain their website. It's all stuff I can easily do, especially with so much time left before the launch, but *thinking* about it is as far as my work has gone. Cece doesn't even know that each day has felt like I'm walking through soup, especially when I avoid all meetings where she has to see my face. No one outside of the employees knows what any of the pastries will be, which adds to the surprise. That part has been fun. Another thing we need to figure out is the floor plan so we can prepare for a large crowd.

Cece wants me there on launch day. Which means Becca will be there. Which means Nichole will be there too.

"Let me just wake up for a second," I respond sleepily, moving to the espresso machine like I'm walking through spaghetti sauce.

"Wake up? Pete, it's noon."

I twist to face her. “It’s noon?!” I hurry to pull out my phone and check the time. My entire screen is blanketed in texts from Cece, asking where I was for our meeting this morning. I bury my face in my hands. “I had a Zoom meeting with Cece three hours ago.”

Kacey puts on a compassionate look. “Okay, this is ridiculous. Go upstairs and take a shower.”

I rummage through the papers all over my kitchen island to find my laptop. “Later. I need to send her a lengthy apology email.”

“I think Fran Drescher can wait five minutes for you to shower.” She gives me a stern look and points upstairs. “Go, and I’ll clean up in here.”

“You don’t have to—”

“Don’t make me count to three,” she interrupts through tight lips.

It’s endearing that she’s being such a mom, even though I’m older than her. “Okay, fine.”

Taking a shower makes me feel better. I trim my beard closer to my face, the way I always have it, lather on the beard oil, and toss my disgusting robe in the hamper. I forgot how good it feels to be clean.

I hate it when my sister’s right.

By the time I come back downstairs in jeans and a long-sleeved black shirt, Kacey’s done all the dishes and opened all the curtains and windows, letting the cool, spring air take the stink out of my house. God, I miss having a cleaning lady.

“That’s the Pete I know,” Kacey says with a proud smile.

"Thank you." I give her a kiss on the cheek. I move to the kitchen island and fire up my laptop. "Maybe I'll actually have a clearer head to care about my job."

"I'll clean your house and take a nap on your orgasmic bed," she offers with zero permission from me. She can sleep in that bed all she wants if she's going to clean my house.

"By all means."

She takes two steps toward the foyer, but pauses and deliberates for a moment. "You know, Nichole's having a hard time too."

I peer at her over the top of my laptop. "Wait. You've been talking to her?"

"Well, we were becoming close friends when you guys were together." She shrugs. "Kaden made friends with my kids. I didn't want to lose that."

"Oh." Part of me wishes she never said anything, but I'm also relieved that Nichole hasn't moved on. I can't imagine guys not asking her out left and right at this point.

Kacey steps closer toward me. "I'm only telling you this because it's not too late to make it right." She shakes her head disappointedly and raises her voice, "How has this breakup not motivated you to do the one thing you should have done *months* ago?"

The last time Danny called, it was a week after Nichole broke up with me. I told him not to call me unless Anna finally agreed to sign the papers. He's held true to his word, but everything's been at a standstill. Anna stopped calling me as well, but she hasn't backed down either. The situation is dead with no resolution whatsoever.

I stare blankly at my screen. "I know you're right. I just . . ."

She flaps her arms exasperatedly. "You just *what*?"

"What does it say about me if I give in?" I shout. Kacey's hardened eyes turn soft, putting on her compassionate look again. "It'll say I'm weak. And that our parents' gift meant nothing. That I'm willing to give it away to solve a problem."

"But leaving things the way they are isn't doing anything either, is it?" She flaps her arms again. "Who cares what she thinks? She's living with someone she didn't know was living with his mother. And she *still* chose him over you."

I don't respond as she approaches my side, patting my shoulder. "It's not going to say you're weak, Petey. It's going to say that you will go to great lengths for those you love, even if it hurts." She presses her cheek against mine. "I think Daddy would say the same thing, and tell you that it's okay."

She kisses me on the temple, then heads back to the stairs, leaving me with heavy things to think over.

Kacey laid everything out in a way I never saw before. Anna chose that life. Her view of me doesn't matter anymore. This debacle has been in a Mexican standoff since last summer. That's way too long. Settling this will let Nichole know what I'm willing to give up for her.

As Han Solo would say, it's time to punch it.

I knock on a door to a basement on a house that could use a paint job. Something as simple as this door already has me missing my house.

"Are you gonna get that, babe?" a man shouts on the other side.

Sounds like a winner.

Footsteps thump closer to the door, and she opens it with an obnoxious creaking noise. She's dressed to stay at home with her oversized sweater and leggings, but she's still wearing makeup. Her bare feet show off her pedicured toes, her hair is tied into a neatly curled bun. Always trying to be pretty and perfect.

"Pete." Anna shuts the door behind her. "What are you doing here?"

I wordlessly hand her a folded piece of paper. She doesn't need to ask what it is when she opens it. The sly smile on her face pisses me off, but I keep my cool. "The deed to the house," she says, holding back the excitement she wants to show.

I shove my hands in my pockets. "You win. It's yours."

"Did that floozy change your mind?"

I pinch my lips together hard enough to hurt. "Sign the papers. *Now.*"

"Happy to." She prances back inside the home, and I have to bite my fist in grief. I'm giving everything up. All of it to put this ugly chapter of my life to rest.

All of it for Nichole.

Anna comes back with the divorce papers. "Here you go."

I flip through the pages to make sure she did actually sign and she's not just screwing with me.

"Well, whaddya know? The Antichrist lives up to her word," I mumble.

"Excuse me?" she sneers.

I don't respond. I curl the papers into a tunnel. "Block my number. Get out of my life. And if you ever, *ever* come after my girl again, I'll take you straight to court, you hoe."

Without waiting for a response, I walk away from her one last time with a smile. Contradictory, considering I gave up my house.

But all that matters is that I feel like a new man.

I gave the papers to Danny right after I got them from Anna. A few days later, he confirmed that the clerk filed them, meaning the marriage is legally over. I'm finally a free man. But as much as I want to jump the gun to get back in Nichole's life, I have a few more things to take care of first.

For the next week, I get everything packed and sent to storage. Everything I didn't take to Goodwill is packed in garbage bags or boxes, and my bedroom furniture is already moved to Kacey's house. It's practically empty now. All that's left to go is me, and my project in the garage.

I take one last look at everything. The kitchen where I did all of my work. The huge TV in the main living room where I watched all my *Star Wars* shows. The front room where I danced with Nichole and Becca. The dining room where Kevin somehow broke through Taryn's quiet nature. The bedroom where I kept all my *Star Wars* costumes. The office where I kept all my valuable collectibles. The other bedroom I used as a gym. The bathroom where Lucas bathed in my cologne. The trimmed backyard with the grill that helped me make steak for Nichole and her friends.

It was a fun bachelor pad while it lasted.

I go back to the garage to the now-empty shelves still covered in paint spatter and dust, and light a cigar. I take a moment to inhale the nostalgic scent, letting it surround me in a mist before I continue with my project. During the last few months of not seeing Nichole, I've been sifting through selfies of us. Before I knew it, I was drawing her—her dark brown skin, the bandana she'd wear when cleaning, elbows propped up and holding a caramel macchiato with the perfect crosshatch caramel drizzle on top, her chocolate eyes looking directly at me. In the background, I'm painting the kitchen the way I saw it when Nichole sat at my island for the first time. She's the reason I got back to doing this; it's only fitting that this is a diorama of her. Dad would be proud. He'd do the same thing.

After working on it for two hours, I go upstairs to my bedroom for the last time. I'm going to miss this place. My heart literally aches.

The crab shells, fish bones, and chunks of canned tuna I plan on shoving into all the curtain rods in the house tomorrow morning makes it less painful.

Caffeinated Vino's coffee side of the lobby is jam-packed. I'm pretty sure the entire town decided to show up. It's so hot that I actually regret wearing long sleeves. The heat from coffee machines and the May sun doesn't help matters.

Despite that, everyone is raving about the new pastries.

"This legit tastes like a mocha!"

"The matcha with banana and brown sugar is so good!"

"The cookies are perfect for my tea!"

I'm glad I told Cece to push the chairs and tables toward the walls as much as possible because the event page was exploding and I had a feeling it was going to be busy. It's caffeinated chaos in here, and some of it has migrated to the bar side of the place.

Becca's working behind the bar, sweating and hyper focused on the drinks. She gives me a shy smile when she sees me talking to people in the lobby. Then she waves me over.

"Just letting you know Nichole plans on being here in a bit," she says.

I shrug. "I figured she would be. Thanks for letting me know, though." I tilt my chin toward her. "Good to see you."

"You too, Pete."

Of course, when I turn around, Nichole walks in. My ex-girlfriend whose hair is now blonde. Everything else is the same, including her Grogu earrings, her *Friends* leggings, bright yellow running shoes, and an oversized shirt with the Mandalorian and Grogu on it.

I told myself I would be okay if she came in. I'm not so sure anymore.

Standing behind a table with samples and a coffee cup in hand, I observe her in line, on her phone, probably scrolling through social media. She always did that when we went somewhere and had to wait. A part of me hopes she'll text me to make sure I'm here. She knew I played a large role in this. She did help me, after all.

She talks to Becca, whose focus is narrowed at the espresso machine. She smiles and laughs, and it's just how I remember it. Throaty, silly, goofy, and plain gorgeous. A dull ache blooms in my chest just seeing her and remembering everything I love about her.

Nichole turns to my table and stills. I wave at her silently with a tight-lipped smile. She breaks her gaze to focus on the floor and slowly steps toward me.

"Hey," she says weakly.

"Hey, Nichole."

Her hands have to find something to do as she takes the corner of her pastry bag and rolls it in her fingers, still not looking at me. "How've you been?"

Terrible. My life is nothing without you in it. "I'm doing okay. You?"

Her head bounces side to side, deliberating. "Same. I'm helping Kaden with putting together his science fair project. I forgot to thank you for your help. It's helped him a lot."

"It was my pleasure." Because she mentioned Kaden, I have to ask. "How's he doing?"

She hums. "He's doing all right."

I want to ask so badly if he misses me, but I can't come across as needy. "What did you get?" I point at the pastry bag in her hand.

She gives me a knowing smile. "What do you think?"

I chuckle. "The caramel macchiato fudge. I should've known."

Her eyes roam the crowd, the bustling coffeehouse, and the staff running around like mad. "You did good. It's a great turnout."

I wink. "All because of your help."

She smiles shyly, as if she doesn't like being reminded of our past. I don't either; it hurts like crazy. All it does is make me miss her so much I can feel my insides tear apart. Then I end up wondering if she misses me the same way.

"I should get going," she says in a near whimper. "Good luck with today."

I raise my hand to bid her farewell. "Bye, Nichole."

I watch her leave, remembering when I'd wrap my arm around that waist, how I'd hold those hands in mine, how her hair felt against my lips when I'd kiss her on the head. How those lips felt.

It'll take some time, but when everything's settled, I'm getting my girl back.

Chapter 24

Nichole

If I've ever thought my dining room table looked like a disaster zone, tonight has put it to a whole new level.

The science fair is in two days. Both Kaden and Oscar have their trifold boards on the table with markers, Sharpies, glue, scissors, and paper pieces strewn everywhere. Some of it ended up on the floor. Yet, I have my Felicias and Knox chipping in to help, with his girlfriend Katie hanging out in the living room. Surprisingly, Knox wasn't opposed to helping kids put projects together, and Katie thought she was crowding the table even more, so she's watching TV.

The school year is almost over. Thankfully, this is the last huge project to do before summer break starts, and then Kaden will be gone visiting Jared for two months starting in July.

"Wow, Felicia," Becca notes as she examines the results on a spreadsheet. "You drank a ton of coffee!"

Taryn shrugs. "It helped me be more productive than energy drinks. Knox gave me a Monster and failed to tell me it was sugar-free." She gags. "It was disgusting!"

Knox chuckles. "I had to mess with you a little bit! You have this strong aversion to anything healthy!"

"Because it's all disgusting!"

Becca takes out her phone to send a text. My phone vibrates on the table.

Becca: I think they're done helping.
Me: ten bucks says Katie will intervene out of jealousy.

I sneak a peek as Becca quickly turns to see what Katie's doing. Watching TV and texting, totally oblivious.

Becca: she doesn't even know what's happening. She's missing out on the love fest that no one will admit to over here.

I shake my head and lay my phone back down on the table.

Stuff like this has been a welcome distraction from thinking about Pete. It doesn't seem like it's been all that long since our breakup, but I miss him something awful. But I've been trying to do what I should've done in the beginning: focus on being Kaden's mom.

It almost made me vomit when I had to tell Kaden the bad news. He shut down completely. Just stared at the TV and refused to talk about it. It shattered my heart that I brought this pain on my boy. I blamed myself for letting Pete meet him so soon.

"That's just part of being a single parent," Taryn had reminded me at a girl's evening. "It's not your fault."

He seems to be doing well, though. He hasn't mentioned Pete or asked about him in quite some time. When Knox walked in earlier this evening, his immediate question was if he was my new boyfriend. I shut that down real quick. Taryn can have him all to herself.

It takes another hour or so for us to finish. Taryn did really well with placing everything on each board so it flowed perfectly. Meticulously drawn arrows point from one step to the other in a beautiful river of information.

"It looks great, guys!" I exclaim, clapping.

"It's because I'm really good at organizing," Taryn brags, then gives Knox the evil eye. "And my results didn't involve sugar-free energy drinks!"

"I believe some of it involved a shot of whiskey in your coffee," he retorts.

Taryn juts out a hip. "You make me sound like an alcoholic!"

He spreads out his arms. "Am I wrong, though?"

Taryn and Knox take their argument to the living room, where Katie can hear and roll her eyes. Becca shrugs and announces she has to head back to her place. Oscar takes his project home while Kaden and I put the trifold board in the back seat of my car. I know myself well enough that we'll bring everything else but the project itself. I'm always doing something or thinking of something.

One of which I wish I could forget.

Science fair day is a busy one. It wasn't till after school, so I had to leave my client's house early to come home and make sure Kaden was showered and changed, then drive back to the school. We meet Oscar and Camilla at the designated table in the school gym to set up everything. I brought a small coffee maker to plug in and serve to people passing by. Soon, the gym is full of families, smiling at each child's presentation.

"Coffee?" I ask to one man passing our table.

"Oh no," he politely declines. "Too late for caffeine."

"It's decaf." I wink.

He shrugs with a satisfied smile and takes the tiny Dixie cup from my hand.

"Was it really decaf?" Kaden leans over to whisper.

I scoff. "Yeah. I'm not a monster." I straighten up and pour another cup for the next guest. "Coffee?"

Over and over again, I watch Kaden and Oscar make their presentation to some very invested parents, gesturing at the chart with Becca's and Taryn's numbers.

And Pete's.

Pete. The man who was sweet enough to help a child that wasn't his succeed. One of the things I loved about him.

Life was brighter when Pete was in it. This breakup has just been a void for me and Kaden. Despite the fact that he lied to me, everything else about him was perfect. Some nights, I crave his beard rubbing my face as he kisses me. That alone has almost caused me to text him, but my resolve wins out every time. Kacey and I stayed in touch because of our kids, but she's also become a good friend to me. I never ask her about Pete. I don't want her to feel like I'm only talking to her to get to him. I don't want him to be the only thing we have in common.

As the hours go by, I don't see Kaden all that excited about his project like he was earlier. His enthusiasm declined pretty quickly. I almost chalk it up to him just being tired. I had the fleeting idea to get some caffeinated coffee to light a fire under his booty. Seeing him bouncing off the walls would be humorous, but also make for a really long night.

But I know my son. The frown on his face isn't one that says he's tired. He shuts down when he's sad about something.

When the fair is over, it takes a few minutes to pack everything and put it in a box. I bid Camilla and Oscar good night, and Kaden barely says anything. He's quiet, sucked into his own world.

"You did a good job tonight, baby."

"Thanks," he replies weakly.

Yep. Something's bothering him.

I lay the poster in the back seat. "You okay?"

Kaden doesn't respond as we get into the car. He still doesn't say anything while we buckle up.

"Did something happen during the fair?"

"No."

"Then what's going on?"

He stares down at his fidgeting hands. I start to think he's not going to open up, then he says, "I wish Pete could've come."

My throat tightens and renders me silent. Kaden hasn't mentioned him in months, yet for some reason, this night reminded him of Pete. The last gift Kaden got from Pete was his results. A silent goodbye.

I think back to everything he did for Kaden. Brought him his favorite toy when he was sick. Helped him bring his imagination to life with *Fortnite* guns. Taught him new pranks (that he thankfully hasn't tested on me . . . yet). Shared a few gallons of Snickers ice cream.

He was Kaden's buddy.

But he ruined it.

"I know," I reply, combing my hand over Kaden's head. "I'm sorry."

I turn on the engine to hide the fact that I can't say anything else on the subject that won't get his hopes up. Because even though Pete screwed up big time, he changed our lives.

He is the best person I've ever known.

That's why I'll never be able to stop loving him.

It's finally Saturday, and I plan on doing absolutely nothing.

Two days after the science fair, I looked through my photo album at old photos of me and Pete. Apparently, I love to torture myself with an ex that I'll never move on from. I didn't fall asleep till one in the morning, trying not to cry over a loss that I feel I should have moved on from already.

"You look like a raccoon," Kaden comments as I get a bowl of cereal ready for him.

"Thanks, that's sweet of you." I look at him sitting at the dining room table, his arms and neck peppered with Sharpie marks from the pen fight he got into with Oscar while Taryn was drawing her perfect arrows. "You're wearing your underwear outside your pants."

Kaden looks down in a panic, then glares at me. I give him an evil grin. "That's what you get." I stick out my tongue at him. "Don't ever call a woman a raccoon."

"Noted."

The doorbell rings as I put the bowl of cereal on the table. Kaden doesn't even notice me opening the door as he chows down on his Froot Loops. On the doormat is a gift basket wrapped with a bright green bow. Beneath the plastic wrapping is a pile of random gifts, some of which are green and brown.

Grogu colors.

I bring the basket inside and tear through the plastic. I smile with each item I pull out, and I know immediately who sent this.

A Grogu mug. A small bunch of fake flowers. A *Star Wars* bandana. A gift card for a coffee roastery. An ugly-as-all-get-out Christmas style sweater of the Battle of Hoth.

Then, last but not least, a card with Han Solo and Leia with cartoon bubbles that say "I love you" and "I know."

Thinking of you. Always.

I cover my mouth with my hand, holding back tears. He hasn't moved on. He hasn't forgotten about me.

"Who's that from?" Kaden asks with a mouthful of cereal.

I can't get his hopes up. It's best not to mention Pete right now, especially since he missed him at the science fair.

I fold up the card. "A friend."

Chapter 25

Nichole

I wish I could say I love dogs. For the most part, I do. However, when a dog decides to take your extendable duster and make it its new chew toy, they're not that great. In fact, they're *definitely* not great when they refuse to give it back, and you have to chase them around the house trying to retrieve the duster. It's even better when the dog's owner does absolutely nothing about it, and just laughs. People are just *awesome.*

Which is why I had to make a trip to Landing Plaza for a new one after my morning run, and I'm *absolutely* including a trip to Caffeinated Vino. At least I can count the duster as a tax write-off.

I get a text as soon as I load the duster into my trunk.

Becca: Sooooo . . . we got some new artwork at the shop.

The ominous way she presents this very random piece of news honestly has me intrigued. For some reason, she thought I might find this interesting. Knowing Becca, her randomness always stems from a valid reason.

Me: Does it have baby dolls coming out of the frame like Phoebe's pictures in Friends?

Becca: Sorry to disappoint, but it's not that creepy. I think you should take a look . . .

Funny how that worked out.

I make my way to Caffeinated Vino, and Becca is waiting for me at the door. Odd. She's *always* too busy to meet me for this kind of thing.

She worries at her bottom lip, almost like she's concerned about my reaction. Ooh. This is serious.

"What? What is it?"

She motions her head to the wall behind the counter. "Look."

It takes me a second to see what she's talking about, but when I do, I can't help but gape at it.

Pete's diorama.

It's me, holding a cup of coffee, peering over the steaming mug of caramel macchiato, topped with the perfect cross-hatch drizzle.

He finished it. He finally finished it.

He took his dad's project and included me in it. He told me he was thinking about what was important to him, and he chose me.

I'm still important to him.

I'm about to cry.

"He brought it by this morning," Becca says. "Cece thought it was so gorgeous and it fit the overall vibe of the place, so she hung it up right after he left."

My throat tightens. The tears start falling when Becca wraps her arm around my shoulders and rubs circles on my back. I'm happy to see that he picked up his old hobby again, which means he's making progress. What about the divorce? Has he done anything with that? If he has, and he still loves me, why hasn't he reached out?

"I miss him," I croak.

She leans her head on my shoulder. "I know you do."

Every day for two weeks, more gifts show up at my door, always with a note from Pete.

One was a crystal cube with a photo of us laser engraved with a note that said: *My favorite photo of us.*

Another one was an original painting of an Ewok holding a lightsaber with the note: *When you wish there was a self-defense course that involves lightsabers.*

On a takeout container with steak and mashed potatoes, he wrote: *This is still my favorite meal of all time, simply because you chose it for me.*

On a bottle of red wine, a sticky note reads: *When you just can't handle Greta anymore.*

I downed the bottle in two days.

On a box of plain pasta, he wrote: *I can't help but laugh every time I go down the pasta aisle.*

To top it off, Becca shows up this morning with a paper cup that I know is a caramel macchiato with his writing on the side: *Hope this takes the edge off a bad day.*

"Did you tell him I had a bad day or something?"

Becca shrugs. "He stopped by the shop and asked about you and whether you saw the diorama. Then told me to personally deliver this to you."

I groan in protest, but I don't hesitate to take the cup from her. "Why is he doing this to me?"

Becca follows me inside and crosses her arms. "Felicia, it's been two long weeks of this. Just take him back! No one else you had a crappy date with put in this much effort." A light bulb goes off in her head when her mouth forms into an O and her eyes go wide. "Unless you're dragging this out to get more stuff?"

I scoff. "Oh please. I miss him, but I can't seem to get over the fact that he lied. Just like Jared did. I can't put them in different categories. I need to stay focused on being Kaden's mom."

Becca hums. "Let's see how long that lasts."

There's a hint of a smile on her face before she closes the door behind her.

On Saturday, I decide to chill out in a ratty T-shirt with paint spatters and Grogu leggings. Kaden went next door to hang out with Oscar, so I have the place to myself for a while. I can't find anything good to watch on TV. I pass over anything that reminds me of Pete. Honestly, everything reminds me of him. Even the home shows and commercials of getting quality products for cheap remind me of Pete and his consistent presents. I flip through channels, and I can't help but wonder with each flicker of the screen why he hasn't reached out to tell me he's divorced. Or what message he's trying to tell me with these gifts.

The doorbell rings and puts an abrupt stop to my thoughts. Dear Lord, tell me it's not another delivery.

A bouquet of carnations and roses explode in color at my doormat. The card attached, right on top, reads clear as day: *You're getting a ride to the beach in five minutes. Get your shoes on.*

I take the bouquet and set it on the table, but stare at the note. I don't know whether to believe this or if it's some funny prank. And the note isn't Pete's handwriting. He must have had the florist do it.

Meh. He has a sense of humor. This has to be a joke. I'll just stay in my sweats and call it good.

That is, until there's a knock on my door five minutes later. This time, a booming one. So, the note was real after all.

I scramble to get my shoes on, then open the door. I cover my mouth and lean over in laughter, because it's two Stormtroopers standing in front of me. Guns and all, although fake.

"We're here to take you to the lake," one of them says in a voice changer, robotic and dry, so I can't identify who's talking.

I hold up my hand while recovering from laughter. "Wait. Hold on."

"I don't recommend you laugh, Jedi," the other one says.

If Pete set this up, he's a genius. "What's happening here? Who are you?"

One of them motions to the car with their fake gun. "Get in."

I have no choice but to follow the Stormtroopers to a car. A silver car. A silver car with a shiny spaceship interior.

Pete's.

One Stormtrooper gets in the back seat with me and the other gets behind the steering wheel. It feels more like a police car than anything now. No one's speaking, and I'm trapped in an enclosed space with enemies. What if they're taking me to a dark dungeon? What if I'm being sold into slavery to Jabba the Hutt? Who's going to take care of Kaden if something happens to me? Dear God, I don't want him going to live with Jared! Why did I get in the car?

"Seriously, what is this? Why do you have Pete's car?"

They say nothing. I can't even focus on the path we're taking because I'm low-key starting to panic. "Will one of you freaking talk?" I snap.

"Will you freaking calm your tits?" the Stormtrooper sitting next to me snaps back.

Okay. These Stormtroopers feel real. They're always mean in the movies, and these people are playing the parts really well.

I take it back. Pete is not a genius.

"Where's Kaden? Is he okay?"

"Your child is in good health with a trusted confidant," the driving Stormtrooper answers.

I don't believe them, but I don't have a choice right now.

We arrive at the beach, and I'm taken back to my first date with Pete, laying in the grass and talking for hours into the night till I was sure my butt turned into a flat pancake. On a warm, sunny day like this, the park is full of people taking a stroll with their partners and dogs. Trees flowing in the soft breeze makes it beautiful, but I can't enjoy it because, well, I'm a willing prisoner.

After parking, we get out of the car. The Stormtroopers aim their fake guns on my back. One of them presses a button on the chest of their suit, and the "March of the Resistance" plays loudly.

Okay. Now this is funny. I snort a laugh, but quickly stop when they force me to start walking. There's literally nothing but strange looks from onlookers. I mean, I'm being shamefully escorted into a park like a prisoner by *Star Wars* enemies with very serious theme music to follow. This isn't exactly a wedding ceremony.

"All is well!" I shout, my voice shrill. I add some hysterical laughter. "Everything's fine! Just a reenactment! They're nice Stormtroopers!"

I'm lying, but I had to throw that in there.

They take me to a space between two trees, right where Pete and I sat. And there, a blanket neatly laid out with two paper coffee cups, is the man I love. My heart leaps to my throat, and I cover my mouth with my hand. It's been a handful of months since I last saw him, but it feels like

I haven't seen him in years with how slowly the time has passed. The same guy that always wears a curve-hugging long sleeved shirt, jeans, and utility boots. I missed those crystal-blue eyes, and his smooth, perfectly trimmed beard that I haven't felt in so long.

Pete turns around and smiles at me, the one I've missed so much. The breeze drags his woodsy, charcoal scent to my nostrils as he stands, and I wonder why I ever broke up with him.

"You can turn that off." He points to the Stormtrooper that I briefly forgot was standing behind me. "You're not taking her to her execution. But thank you."

They lay their guns on the grass, give him a deep bow like he's Emperor Palpatine, then walk away.

I'm breathless. "Pete . . . what—what's going on?"

He doesn't respond. Instead, he sits back down on the blanket and pats the space next to him. Hesitant, I sit beside him. He hands me a folded paper.

Can't be more test results.

I open it and take a moment to examine the form that says "Decree of Dissolution of Marriage" and two signatures on it.

Not just his. Hers. Anna's.

He got a divorce.

He gave up his house.

"I was waiting till it was final before I set all this up," he fills me in. "I didn't want to restart something before I knew for sure that everything was done."

I gape at the paper, then back at him. "So, you're officially divorced? You . . . gave her the house?"

Pete nods with his lips clenched together. “I did.” His eyes squeeze shut, crinkling at the corners. “I thought it was the hardest thing I’d ever have to do. But when I realized the hardest thing was being without you, it suddenly became much easier to stop playing Anna’s game. I’d give up everything if it meant I got to be with you.” He takes a breath. “I moved in with Kacey, and I’m saving to get a place of my own.” He twists his body to face me, bringing a hand to my cheek and lovingly stroking it. Oh, have I missed his touch. So much so that I can’t help myself when I reach forward and stroke his beard. My fingertips gently roam his jawline, his lips, his scalp.

“You gave it all up for me,” I say, still in disbelief. “What changed?”

He smiles. “My sister.”

“God, I love your sister.”

Pete chuckles. “I was more afraid of appearing weak by giving in. She helped me to see that by giving in, I’d be doing it for someone I love, even if it hurts.”

“If only you’d done it—”

Pete holds up a hand to stop me. “Please don’t bring up how much better it would’ve been if I just listened.”

I shrug. “Just sayin’.” My old worries come rushing back. I need him to say it. “You never forgot about me?”

He scoffs at the ridiculousness. “You’re the only thing I’ve thought about for all these months.”

My smile grows wider. “Me too.”

He takes my face and leans his forehead against mine. His thumbs roam back and forth over my cheeks. “I never, ever, ever wanna be apart from you that long again.”

“I don’t either.”

Pete smashes his lips on mine in a searing kiss, the softness of his beard tickling my chin the way I love so much. “I love you.”

I wink. “I know.”

He brings me in for another kiss, gentler this time. It’s cut way too short when we hear loud, girly cheering behind us. When I turn to find the reason why we stopped kissing, I see the Stormtroopers jumping up and down with their helmets off.

Becca and Taryn.

“Are you serious?!” I shriek and smack Pete on the shoulder. “What did you do to get them to do this?”

Pete shrugs like it’s nothing. “Whiskey and cash.”

“Did you rehearse all this?”

His mouth lifts at the corner. “I’m nothing if not prepared.” He motions to my friends. “I had to train them on how to use those suits.”

“Of course. I should’ve known.” I rub my nose against his. “Thank you.”

Becca and Taryn race over to us. It’s a round of hugs and congratulations and tears. The tears, of course, are from me.

Taryn waves a hand in her face. “These suits are so freaking hot.”

“Yeah, we did our duty and we’re dying.” Becca holds out a hand. “It’s payday.”

Pete laughs joyfully and slaps some bills in her hand. "Thank you. Thank you both."

"Okay, we don't wanna see y'all makin' out, so we're gonna go." Taryn takes Becca's arm and they leave us alone.

Pete gives me that heart-stopping smile before he returns to kissing me. As I cherish his perfect lips, I revel in how right everything feels now. He was the void I was missing this whole time.

All because I decided to trust him.

Epilogue

Pete

"Did you really have to wait for the hottest day of the year to move?" Taryn whines as she lifts another box from my storage unit into a large moving truck. I got my own place, at last.

Kind of. I'm moving in with Nichole.

"They just wanna start making babies in the privacy of their own home," Kacey comments.

"Ew!" Kaden covers his ears and starts babbling nonsense.

Nichole and I got married at the beginning of July, right before Kaden left to visit with his dad. Becca was Nichole's maid of honor with Taryn as the bridesmaid, and Kaden walked Nichole down the aisle. Kevin was my best man, with Lucas as my little groomsman. Neither one of us wanted a big wedding for our second wedding, and it was everything we ever dreamed of.

Our cake was a Death Star, and Anakin and Padmé Amidala were the cake toppers. Sue me.

"Well better that than Kacey's basement," Becca mumbles, to which I vigorously agree.

I glance at my watch. "Oh, babe, we should probably get ready to take Kaden to the airport."

"But-but-but," she sputters in a whine. She told me how hard it is when she sends Kaden to see his dad. I had to reassure her that she doesn't have to go through that alone anymore. It bothers me that she was by herself during those times, even though Becca and Taryn live above her. "Can't we wait a little longer? We still have a few more boxes left."

I come to her side and give her a kiss on the head.

"Nah, we got it," Kacey offers.

Taryn leans in close to Nichole's ear, saying through clenched teeth, but loud enough for me to hear, "You're going to have the whole summer to yourself. Just you. And. Him."

Yeah. That perks her right up. "Okay, honey, you're right, let's go."

"Do you have your bag, bud?" I ask Kaden. He and I have become super close since I came back into their lives. Us getting married was almost the best day of his life.

"Yup, it's in the car," he answers, wiping the sweat off his forehead.

"Thank you for helping, you guys!" Nichole hugs her friends and Kacey, and even hugs Lucas and Charlotte. "Let us know if there's more to be done once we leave the airport."

We're acting as if we're never going to see each other again. The girls hug Kaden too, even though I've realized he's not much of the hugging type. At our wedding, he patted Nichole on the head after walking her down the aisle, and just walked off.

At the airport, I help get Kaden's suitcase out of the back seat. Nichole embraces him one more time, totally dreading this moment. Even I get a little emotional.

"I love you, baby." She plants a kiss on his head.

"Love you, Mom."

I don't plan on hugging him. I'm his buddy. The cool stepdad. We're in the stage of mature handshakes and high fives.

"Be safe, okay?" I say, holding out my hand.

Kaden doesn't take it. He looks up at me, but not because he's judging me. The wheels are turning in his mind. We don't have a signature handshake or anything, so I'm not sure what he's deliberating.

He answers the question for me when he does something I didn't expect in the slightest.

He hugs me.

I still for a second, trying to make sure this is really happening. When I look up at Nichole bracing her cheeks and her eyes are twinkling, I know it's real. I'm getting choked up.

I'm the recipient of Kaden's rare hugs.

Just think. A year ago, I never saw myself being a father in any way. I didn't think I'd find someone who understood me as well as Nichole does. I found her in a coffee shop, and everything else turned into one fast, beautiful blur.

All the sacrifices were worth it.

Thanks so much for reading *Cleanup on Aisle Geek*! I hope it made you laugh and warmed your heart.

Want more of the Felicias? Keep reading for a sneak peek of Taryn's story in *Misery on the Rocks*!

Taryn and Knox are best friends, and that's all. At least, that's how it seems. Despite things never going her way, Knox is always there. Eventually, she'll have to see that something good is right in front of her. Right?

Oh, and if you enjoyed this read, pretty please leave a review on Amazon, Goodreads, Barnes & Noble, or StoryGraph, as it helps more readers find my books!

Follow me on:
Facebook: Sarah Blynne Writes
Instagram: @sarahblynnewrites
TikTok: @sarahblynne

Acknowledgments

This book was so fun to work on! It's so different from the fantasy series I wrote since I could add my own sass, spunk, and modern lingo. It's even better when you have real people in your life that inspire the characters.

I want to thank my best friends, Amanda and Tally, for being the inspiration for the humor in this book and the upcoming books. You guys have never failed to make me laugh and be the support I've always needed. Also, thank you so much to my friends Chelsea and Knicole for taking the time to read this and give me valuable feedback. Also my editor, Kasey, who absolutely rocks at her job. And Caiti for giving the business boost I've needed. Of course, I will always thank my parents, Francine and Alex, for supporting my author career and for also giving me helpful feedback.

And, as always, I save the best for last, my husband Cody. It means so much to me that you support me not only because you're my husband, but because you truly want to. I love you for that.

See you in the next book!

Sarah Blynne

More from the Author

<u>Romance</u>

Bloom

<u>Fantasy</u>

The Call of Thunder (Hidden Heroes Book 1)

The Call of Allies (Hidden Heroes Book 2)

The Call of Freedom (Hidden Heroes Book 3)

Keep reading for a preview of

Misery on the Rocks

By

Sarah Blynne

Chapter 1

Taryn

I, Taryn Mendes, hereby declare that my life has always involved being a third wheel, working with stupid people, and other minor issues that were super inconvenient but just accept it as a part of my life.

If I were to write a letter alongside my will, that's how it would start. Because it's true. My best friend's girlfriend gets on my nerves. I'm always the third wheel. I don't get along with my mom. My flights always somehow get delayed. And, my most recent problem: My boss is a moron. Half the time, I'm doing her work on top of my own, yet *she*'s the HR manager.

Story of my life.

But I try (*try* is the key word here) to remember the good things I still have. Even though my best friend, Knox, has a girlfriend, we still hang out all the time. My other best friends, Becca and Nichole, live in the same fourplex as I do in Creekside. Nichole's been busy the last three months enjoying wedded bliss with her husband Pete, but she's still heavily involved in our group chat. I started dating Pete's business partner, Kevin, right after Nichole's wedding, and it's been pretty great. He doesn't mind when I hang out with

Knox, and sometimes he'll even join us. He's usually busy with work, so I end up being the third wheel again.

I don't mind when he works. He always wears an impeccable suit with a shirt open at the collar. Hubba-hubba.

I wish he was on this date with me, though, because Katie is making a show of who Knox belongs to. Creekside isn't that big, and Caffeinated Vino is the only coffee shop and bar in the area. *Everybody* knows who belongs to her.

She's squished so close to him in the booth she may as well be putting her bony butt in his lap. Knox gives a tight-lipped smile, one that he seems to mainly use on her. I know him; he's not crazy about this showy display, but he likes her, so he's allowing it. They're usually this disgusting anyway, whether Kevin's with me or not. Katie's kicking it up a notch because I'm the only one here.

I sneak a text to my Felicias.

Me: Someone bring me a bucket. This is making me want to vomit.

We became Felicias (name based on a common phrase a few years ago that we randomly started calling each other) when me, Becca, and Nichole all wanted the same available apartment in the fourplex we live in now. Nichole told us the heart-wrenching story about being a single mom and going through a divorce, so we decided she wins in the pity category and let her have the apartment. It was a miracle that two more apartments opened up in the same fourplex that Becca and I snatched in a heartbeat.

Becca: You know you don't have to be the third wheel. You already know Katie is a snob. This is on you.

Me: This seems to be the only time I can hang out with Knox this week. He's been slammed at the restaurant.

"So where's your man, Taryn?" Katie asks as she whips her Barbie-blonde head in my direction. Her bright white smile just screams fake. She just wants to rub it in my face that Knox is hers.

Yeah. I know. I hear you loud and clear.

"Working," I say dryly before sipping my whiskey sour. I should've added another shot in this drink.

You love Knox. You're doing this because he's your best friend and he's always been there for you. Just keep sucking it up.

Katie puts on a grouchy face. "It seems like he's always working." She shifts her gaze at Knox like he's her whole world. "I think it would be hard if you were always working. We'd never see each other."

Wow. Needy much?

"I'll always make time for you, sweetie," Knox assures her in his low, Southern drawl.

Katie purrs. "I love your accent."

Now she's making out with him. She's trying way too hard to put on a show.

Oh, My*lanta*. This is so awkward. Take me away, Lord.

My phone flashes with a text from Kevin. Thank God.

Kevin: Hey honey, I'm done with work. I can meet at your place if you want. Mom would love to see you too.

Me: Yes. You're officially saving my life.

I shove my phone in my purse and pack up at the speed of light. I'd very much rather hang out with my boyfriend and his mother than watch this public sex show happening before me.

Knox has the self-control to tear himself from Katie's frog lips to watch me. "You heading out?"

I feign being disappointed. "Yeah. Kevin got off work and he's gonna meet me at my place."

"He can always meet us here and hang out," he suggests.

"I'm sure they wanna spend time alone," Katie says in a high-pitched voice, then aims her steely gaze directly at me. "We've already taken enough of Taryn's time, haven't we?"

Again, I hear you loud and clear. You don't want me here. You don't ever want me here. "It's fine. I'll see you guys later."

Katie says "Buh-bye" with a little finger wave at the same time Knox says "See ya, Tar." As I walk to the door, I watch her give him a dirty look. I groan. She doesn't like it when he calls me "Tar." I'm not sure why; it's not like he's calling me "babe" or "hot stuff."

Even if he did . . . ew. He's like the brother I never had. That's never going to happen.

After each time I hang out with them, I never understand why Knox is with her. They've been together for about a year, and it just doesn't make sense. He's chill, resilient, and open to anything, while she's high-maintenance, insecure, and just plain phony. It's like he's desperate to just have someone.

My cowboy boots clunk on the wooden stairwell on the way to my apartment. My black, long-haired cat, Kitten, sits on the windowsill and watches me with those bright green eyes.

"Yes, Mama's home," I coo as I open the door. She immediately jumps off and rubs herself all over my legs. My cat is the closest thing I have to a child. I love my cat more than life itself.

That's one other great thing I have.

My apartment is full of dim lighting. I've hung up colored lights along my living room wall that is completely full of framed photos of me with all my friends from my hometown in Roswell, New Mexico. I even have photos stuck under the glass of my coffee table. On a beam between the living room and kitchen, there's a banner from my goodbye party from home. I live in memories.

I wander into the playpen-sized kitchen and see what I can feed Kevin and his mom from the fridge. I can't stand leftovers—no thanks to my mom who refused to cook a single thing till leftovers were completely finished—so I don't have much to offer.

A knock on the door interrupts my pathetic search for cooked food. I open the door to Kevin holding two small grocery bags with his mom, Lisa, standing beside him with a bright smile and her short, platinum-blonde hair pushed back with a headband.

"Hey, honey." He leans in and kisses me, his light stubble rubbing against my lips. He's hot and a great kisser; I can't complain about that.

"Hi, sweetheart!" Lisa bends down just a tad to my level and loops me in for a hug. I love Lisa's hugs. I never got enough of these as a kid. I forgot how much I crave it at thirty-seven. "Thanks for having us over!"

I close the door behind us. "Thank your son for texting me. You gave me an excuse to leave Knox's date."

Kevin chuckles as he sets everything on the counter. "Were they getting mushy?"

"She was. He was just going with it."

Lisa scoffs. "Manipulative b—"

"Mom," Kevin barks, which makes me laugh, then addresses me with an apologetic look.

"Well, that's my first impression." She lays her oversized purse on the kitchen counter. "I gotta use the bathroom."

Kevin waits for her to be out of earshot before saying, "I don't get why he doesn't tell her to chill out."

I shrug. "She's insecure."

"Because you're there?"

"Maybe."

He looks at me conspicuously. "I feel like women act like that when they believe their partner has feelings for their girl friends."

"Kev, we've talked about this." I hug his arm and lean my head against his bicep, giving him my best puppy dog eyes. "I've known Knox for *years* and I ain't never felt an inkling of anything."

"I know, I just . . ." He sighs heavily. "Usually, guys and girls who are best friends don't always stay *just* friends, ya know." He turns to grasp my hips. "I'd be lying if I said it didn't cross my mind."

I shake my head and wrap my arms around his neck. "You ain't got nothing to worry about. I promise."

I give him an intense, heartfelt kiss to let him know how serious I am.

I *am* being serious. Knox has always been my best friend and nothing more. He's the only reason I tolerate Katie. And tolerate is a generous word.

"You could always double-date more with me."

"I'll definitely try." He kisses me again. "I miss hanging out with you." He pecks me on the lips one more time, then Lisa comes out of the bathroom. "Let's watch a movie we've seen a million times. It's that kind of day."

Kevin yawns, and I immediately feel bad that he's so tired. "Good idea. I don't want to think anymore."

As we head to the couch in the living room, my phone vibrates in my back pocket. I'm glad I have a glass of whiskey in my hand, because my mom decided to send me a message.

Mother: Call me.

Sounds just like Ruth Mendes. Telling me what to do with no regard as to whether I want to or not.

Lisa must see the expression on my face, because she grasps my bicep. "Everything okay?"

I turn off the screen and put my phone on the counter. Out of sight, out of mind. "Just my mom."

Lisa waves a hand and scoffs. She knows all about her. I told her many, many, many stories about her over dinner with Kevin's family. I rarely talk to people I don't know. It takes a few hangouts to feel like I can be myself. When I do, it's because I'm in a free, safe environment where I get good, trusting vibes from the people I'm with. That's how I connected with my Felicias so well and so quickly.

The same thing happened with Lisa. She had a motherly air to her that sucked me right in. She didn't pressure me to come out of my quiet self; she just gave me space and let me be comfortable in my environment. Then she asked me a question about my living situation. I told her about how I live in a fourplex with my best friends as neighbors, and how they're basically my family, and it all came pouring out from there. She listened, held my hand, and hugged me. Since then, she's been the mother I never had.

"Deal with that later." She waves in dismissal.

I chuckle. She understands. And I will do anything I can to keep her in my life.

People are supposed to believe that working for Tacker Machinery is a great job and you'll be set for life working here. Great pay, great benefits, paid vacation and sick time, the works. Enticing, right?

Then they come in, see how Carolyn Bassett is as a manager, then put in their two weeks after a month, tops. I would be among those people if the pay wasn't worth it. I don't put on slacks and a button-up blouse for fun.

"Carolyn?" I knock on her office door. Her dark blonde hair is in a tight librarian updo, a pair of glasses sit on a large nose, her lips lacquered with a deep red, and her leathery hands are home to a gaudy ring on each finger. The entire getup screams cold and ignorant.

She turns to me with a too-white, fake smile. "Hi, Taryn. What can I do for you?"

"I just want to make sure you know you have an interview with Justin Stokes this afternoon for a mechanic position."

Carolyn taps her desk and hums. I've seen this too many times, and I know what's coming. "I'm not able to make it. I have a meeting I absolutely have to attend later. Can you do the interview for me?"

I'm just a recruiter. I screen people when I call them, but it's not in my job description to actually perform the in-person interviews. As far as I'm concerned, recruiters aren't qualified for that. Yet, I end up doing it all the time. "I emailed you to put it on your calendar," I say dryly, as I have a million times.

"I know and I had to choose between the interview and this meeting because they're both at the same time. I'm sorry. You can do the interview." She winks. "You're good for it."

Would've been helpful if you told me that before I wasted time emailing you about it. "Sure," I reply with clenched teeth, and walk away before I can growl and pounce on her with my claws out.

I need coffee. I got here fifteen minutes ago and I'm already dealing with a truckload of stupid.

Simon's already there at the coffee station, a full mug in hand, holding it out to me. He looks better than I do with his Clark Kent hair and perfectly ironed dress shirt and gray slacks.

"I figured you might need this," he says, while holding his own steaming mug of happiness.

"You know me too well." I take the coffee and grab three pods of creamer. "Carolyn's bailing on me again for the interview today. Says she has a meeting to go to at the same time." I growl. "Would've been nice if she told me."

"Have we ever known Carolyn to tell anyone anything?" Simon pushes his thick-rimmed glasses up his nose. "Thankfully, she leaves me alone to do my job."

"You're the benefits specialist. She don't know nothing about that. Of course she'd leave you alone."

Simon lifts an eyebrow to agree with me. "And John's here more than she is. Not sure what meetings she's attending with him."

"She probably books them a hotel room and she ends up going by herself 'cause he forgot."

Simon snorts mid-sip. "Poor, useless, horny wife."

I wince. "Please don't use horny when describing Carolyn."

He glances at the ceiling in thought. "Yeah, that was in poor taste, wasn't it?"

I laugh as I take my mug with me. "Just pray for me, 'kay?"

Simon presses his hands together in the "namaste" gesture and lightly bows. I don't know what I'd do without him as my confidant. His sanity and laid-back nature are the only things keeping me sane.

About the author

Sarah hails from Tacoma, WA, where she began writing at the ripe young age of eleven. Her writing is inspired from real-life experiences, music, and her own wild imagination.

In her spare time, she enjoys reading, cooking, trying different restaurants, playing video games, going on walks, spending time with her friends and family, and her cat, Gracie, and drinking coffee from anyone who will give it to her.

Her first published young adult romance, *Bloom*, won a Literary Global Book Award in 2025.

Made in United States
Troutdale, OR
09/19/2026

54427441R00163